A mutter is starting in our section. Uneasy, fearful voices.

'Hot . . . '

'It's very hot in here—'

'Too hot—'

'I can't breathe.'

'There's no air.'

'Can't get my breath.'

Someone starts to cry. I don't know what to do. Should I say my bit about it all being part of the ride again? Is anyone going to believe me this time?

And then a thin, high, panicky voice from the end of the section shouts, 'Get us out of here! Are you listening? Get us out of here!'

Also available by Helen Dunmore,
for younger readers:

GO FOX

Helen Dunmore

Yearling Books

FATAL ERROR
A CORGI YEARLING BOOK: 0 440 86345 7

First publication in Great Britain

PRINTING HISTORY
Yearling edition published 1996

Set in 12/15pt Century Schoolbook by
Phoenix Typesetting, Ilkley, West Yorkshire.

Yearling Books are published by Transworld Publishers Ltd,
61–63 Uxbridge Road, Ealing, London W5 5SA,
in Australia by Transworld Publishers (Australia) Pty Ltd,
15–25 Helles Avenue, Moorebank, NSW 2170,
and in New Zealand by Transworld Publishers (NZ) Ltd,
3 William Pickering Drive, Albany, Auckland.

Made and printed in Great Britain
by Cox & Wyman Ltd

For Tess

One

The queue goes all the way back to the sign which says *One hour wait from here*. The words are red on a background of silver stars, and there's a little kid leaning against it with her eyes shut. How's she ever going to queue for another hour? She must have been waiting ages already. She looks about seven or eight. It seems like a hundred years since I was a little girl like that, though really it's only about four.

But we've got a new ride, *SPACE RANGER*. That's why she's come here, and so have thousands of others, kids and adults. They've all heard about it. Last week it was on TV, with a computer expert explaining how the effects worked. He got it wrong, though. Nobody except Virgil and Bella knows how *SPACE*

RANGER works. Not even me, and I live here.

The first coaches rumbled into the car park at seven, full of school parties. I heard the hiss of their air brakes and that horrible beep-beep-beep noise they make when they reverse, but I didn't look out of our trailer window. I was counting last night's money. You have to concentrate. If you take your eyes off the notes, you have to start all over again. A tenner looks like a twenty pound note when your eyes get tired, and then there are the fifties which might be forged. We've got a scanner to check for forgeries at the pay booth, but I always check again when I'm counting the cash. I hold the notes up to the light. When I've counted them I check the total, then Virgil checks it again. And then he goes off with the money. Not to a bank, I know that. Virgil doesn't believe in banks, and nor does Bella. He peels off enough money to keep us going for the week and slides it into a drawer in the fridge, then the rest disappears with him. We always keep our money in the fridge. When I first came to live with the Damianos I used to wonder why. I asked Virgil and he said, 'In case it goes off.'

But who's going to come in here and steal our money? There's always Zorro lying on the grass near the caravan steps, yawning and showing his big red mouth full of teeth. I know Zorro's really friendly, but you wouldn't think so if you didn't know him. I was frightened of him at first. But then I was only about eight. When I first came to live here, Bella made Zorro sniff my hand so he knew me and wagged his tail when he saw me, instead of growling like he does at strangers.

Now I snap my fingers at Zorro. 'Here, boy! Want a walk?'

Zorro always wants a walk. We can't let him run around during the day, because of the Daisies. They get frightened. So I hook his lead onto his collar and he bounds along beside me as we go to have another look at the queue. The little girl is still there but she's moved up the queue a bit. I duck under the barrier, showing my *SPACE RANGER STAFF* badge to the man behind before he starts moaning. The little girl smiles at Zorro and puts out her hand, but her mum sees her and screeches, 'Dinah! Don't go near that horrible dog! He'll bite you!'

'He won't,' I say, but the mum glares at me.

'Dogs like that in a place like this; it shouldn't be allowed,' she snaps. Zorro whines and looks sad.

'He lives here,' I say. And you're only a Daisy, I think, but I don't say it. You don't call them Daisies to their face. Daisy means Day Visitor – and a lot of other things as well.

'He's called Zorro, and I'm Nicky,' I tell the little girl.

'He's a magic dog,' she says, as if she knows all about Zorro.

'Don't be so silly, Dinah,' says her mum. 'Magic! What a load of old rubbish.'

Zorro stares hard at Dinah's mum. He is big and black and wild and he can make himself look even bigger and blacker and wilder when he wants to. Fierce sparks shoot from his eyes. Dinah's mum turns away quickly and pretends to be looking at the ice-cream van. 'I don't know what's so special about this *SPACE RANGER*,' she sniffs. 'It'd better be worth the money, that's all.'

'It is,' I say to Dinah. 'You wait and see.'

'Has he been on it?' she asks, pointing at Zorro.

''Course he has. Well, he has once, before it opened to the public.'

'I've got a brother,' whispers Dinah as if it's a secret.

'Where is he? Is he here?'

She looks around. 'No. He's in hospital. But he's coming home soon. Really soon.' She whispers so her mum won't hear. Maybe her mum doesn't like talking about the boy because he's in hospital.

'How old's your brother?' I ask.

'Twelve.'

'Same as me. What's his name?'

'Steve.'

'Where's the hospital?'

'Near here. We live near here. We're going to see him after. I've got to tell him what it's like on *SPACE RANGER*. He really wanted to come but the doctor said he couldn't.'

Suddenly Dinah looks miserable. I shouldn't have asked her about her brother. Now she isn't having a good time any more. Quickly I say, 'Shall I tell you about *SPACE RANGER*?'

'Don't go spoiling it for her, mind,' cuts in Dinah's mum.

I'd like to get Zorro to chase her right round the theme park and out of the gates screaming, but I don't. Instead I stick a smile on my face and say, 'You can't spoil it by talking about it.' Then I turn to Dinah.

'You start off on the launch pad. You're strapped in, of course. The next moment you feel the engines starting up. You ever been on a plane?' She shakes her head. I don't tell her that I haven't either. 'It's much more powerful than that. You're pinned to your seat. Then there's a massive boost of the engines and you're launched into space. You see the planets whirling outside the window. You can look out and see the Earth. All the seas and the land and everything. If you had a telescope you could see the cities. If you had a mega-telescope you could even see us. There are millions and millions and millions of stars. Soon the Earth is so far away you can't even see it. You're way out in space, sliding down the Milky Way and then out of the galaxy. It's like a jungle of stars. You don't know where you are. You don't know if you'll ever see Earth again.'

'Will I ever come back?' asks Dinah.

''Course you will. Everyone comes back. I mean, you couldn't go and live out in space, could you?'

'I don't want to go on my own.'

'Your mum's going with you.'

'Oh, no, I most certainly am not, young lady,' says Dinah's mum. 'You can get that idea right out of your head. I'm not getting myself all messed up on a space ride. You go on your own or you don't go at all.'

Dinah looks as if she's going to cry. I bend down and pretend to be tightening Zorro's collar. 'It's OK. I'll come with you. Don't tell your mum.'

Dinah beams a huge smile.

So now I'm stuck with it. I just hope Virgil and Bella aren't looking for me. But Bella said I could have a day off after counting the money. Usually I work on the gates or else I help out on one of the other rides if they're busy. You all have to help each other out in a theme park. I look at the queue. It's about half-an-hour long now. I might as well wait here.

Dinah's mum bends down and rubs one of her feet. 'Ooh, this standing around's killing my feet,' she says. She stares at the sign for the café. 'I could murder a cup of tea.'

'Go on, Mum, I'll be all right.'

'I couldn't leave you.'

'Nicky'll look after me, won't you, Nicky?'

'Um, yeah, all right. Yeah, 'course I will.'

Her mum gives me a look as if she's the one who's doing me a favour. 'You sure that dog's OK?' she asks.

'Here, boy,' I say. I bend down and put my hand right in Zorro's mouth. I can feel his hot breath against my skin. Dinah's mum's mouth drops open. 'There. See. He never bites anyone he knows. And he knows Dinah now.'

'Oh, well, all right then. Just for ten minutes. Be a good girl, Dinah.'

'Yes, Mum.'

I wonder if she's Dinah's real mum. She's not at all like her. It might be like me and the Damianos. Because we have the same name, everyone thinks Bella and Virgil are my mum and dad. I didn't used to be called Nicky Damiano, though. When I lived with Dad I was called Nicky Bellos. Only then Dad got the virus. I didn't even know what a virus was.

'It's like when that virus got in the computer, Nicky,' Dad said. 'You remember how it stopped all the programs working? Every time we tried it just flashed up *A fatal error has occurred in the system*. You couldn't play your games and I couldn't do my work.'

It was a people virus that Dad had. It stopped him working bit by bit. One day he couldn't walk me to school. I didn't know then that he'd never be able to walk me to school again. After that, one of my friends' mums used to call for me. I was seven then. The next thing the virus did was stop Dad working. After that it made him go into hospital, just for a few days the first time, then longer. By that time I was staying with friends more than I was at home. There was only Dad and me, we didn't have any other family. That was when Dad wrote to Virgil and Bella. Virgil and Bella and Dad used to work together in computers, inventing computer games, then my dad moved into another job and Virgil and Bella started to invent huge computerized theme park rides. They went to live in a theme park a long way away so we didn't see them much. But Dad said they were the kind of friends you could count on if you were in trouble.

And we were in trouble. Bad trouble. The virus was doing something to Dad's legs now, so he couldn't walk properly. One day when I was in the hospital playroom, Bella Damiano walked in. She was dressed in a long, sky-coloured coat and she had an enormous bunch of grapes on a silver plate. No-one else in the hospital had so many grapes.

'Your dad doesn't want these. Maybe you can help me out,' she said. So we sat and ate grapes and Bella told me without actually saying it that Dad wasn't going to be with me too much longer. I knew it already.

'That's our dog outside the window,' said Bella, and pointed. It was Zorro, tied to a hook outside the hospital door because they hadn't let him in. 'He likes kids. He'd like you. D'you want to come and give it a try? If you don't like us we can think of something else.'

Bella talks about Dad a lot. She and Virgil tell me about things all three of them used to do when they were young. They talk about when

I was a baby and when Dad swam the length of Lake Windermere with his swimming club, before the virus got him. They don't have a special voice for talking about Dad, the way some of my teachers do if I ever say anything about him in school. Once I told the class about how Dad swam right across a lake with me on his back. I wore a wetsuit and held on to his shoulders. It was true but the teacher looked at me as if it was a story I'd made up because Dad was dead and so no-one could know if it was true or not.

'What a good story, Nicky! I bet a lot of us would like to have a dad like that, wouldn't we?'

Yuck.

I jump. Dinah is pulling at my hand. I'd forgotten all about her.

'OK, Dinah. Only about ten minutes to go.'

But Dinah pulls my hand again, more urgently. 'Nicky!'

'What?'

'That man!'

'Who?'

'Over there.'

I look where she's looking. But he must have seen me because he turns away quickly. He doesn't want me to see his face. But I know that back. I'm sure of it. I look away again, pretending not to have noticed anything, and wait a minute, then I slide my eyes sideways. Yes. I thought so. It's him.

'Who is it, Nicky? Why's he staring at you? I don't like him.'

Nor do I, I think. But I say, 'Oh, he's nothing, Dinah. Nothing to worry about.'

We're nearly at the turnstile. I can't break out of the queue now, after Dinah's been waiting so long. But I've got to warn Bella and Virgil. I'm sure it's *him*. One of the Crowleighs. I wouldn't forget those eyes. They're blue and cold and empty and they seem to suck all the warmth out of you as they stare. It's a summer day but he's wearing a heavy leather jacket and a scarf wrapped round his neck. His hands are deep in his pockets. Why's he here? What's he come for this time? And is he the only one here today, or are the others here too, scattered around the theme park, watching and waiting? I've got to warn Bella and Virgil but the crowd is pushing me on, sweeping me up against the turnstile. There's a post behind the booth where I can tie up Zorro. He'll wait till I come back. He won't mind, he's used to it. Ahead of me there's the dark and the glitter of stars. I can hear the roar of *SPACE RANGER*.

Two

Oh, no. Joe Marr's standing at the entrance to *SPACE RANGER*, with his arms folded and a big scowl on his face. He never looks like that with Virgil and Bella. It's all smiles then, as if he really likes them and being in Mere Park and working on *SPACE RANGER*. But I don't think he does. He's always shouting at kids. And he certainly doesn't like me, I know it, though he pretends he does when Virgil or Bella are around. And he pretends he likes Zorro, too, but Zorro knows better. When he sees Joe Marr he growls, a tiny rasping growl deep down in his throat. You can't hear it but I can feel it when I'm holding his collar. I bend down to tie him up to the post.

Joe's been working for us since April. He takes the money and makes sure no-one goes on the ride if they've got a heart condition or anything like that. Virgil and Bella are busy all day in their workshop, inventing the next ride, the new one, the one that everyone'll be talking about next year. Nobody knows what it is yet. They never talk about it, not even to me. The workshop is double-locked and there is only one set of keys.

In some theme parks you pay your money at the entrance and then you can go on all the rides as much as you want, but it's not like that with us. Our rides don't belong to Mere Park. People have to pay extra to go on them. Virgil says the owners of Mere Park offered him twenty thousand pounds to build *SPACE RANGER* here. Twenty thousand pounds! The owners knew that if we took *SPACE RANGER* and our other rides anywhere else, all the Daisies would follow us.

'Wow, twenty thousand pounds! Can I see it, Virgil?'

'We didn't take it.'

'*You didn't take it?* Why not? Why didn't you—'

'No, Nicky. Once someone gives you that much money, he thinks he owns you. Nobody owns us.'

Nobody owns us. I liked the sound of that.

But I liked the sound of twenty thousand pounds, too . . .

'What're *you* doing here?' asks Joe Marr, as if it's any of his business what I do.

'Going on *SPACE RANGER*,' I say.

'What do you want to do that for? You been on it dozens of times.'

'I like it,' I say, and Zorro's growl rumbles softly in his throat. I don't know if Joe Marr hears it, but he shrugs and says, 'OK. Suit yourself.'

'I will,' I say, and I go past Joe to the entrance tunnel. Dinah is right behind me.

Yes, I've been on *SPACE RANGER* loads of times. But each time my heart bumps when it goes dark. The rocket head rises and we move smoothly down the rails. Then it begins. The engines roar and rumble and the capsule judders and I feel the lift under me as the rocket starts its long soar into space. Gravity presses me down into my seat and I shut my eyes, counting the seconds. Then I open them again. I look out of the window and see a blur of sky, then clouds. The engines thunder as we rip through the cloud cover and out into the darkness of space. Suddenly it's silent, magical, floating, then the engines thrust again and we are out of orbit, heading away from the safe circle of earth into deep space. Earth glow falls through the window onto our faces. Dinah's eyes are tight shut, her hands grasping the arm rests.

'Look, Dinah! Look!'

Slowly she opens her eyes. Her face is screwed up with fear. Then she sees the blue and green globe of Earth through the window, floating away from us, and her face goes smooth with amazement.

'What's that thing, Nicky?'

'It's Earth. Our Earth.'

Is it real or isn't it? One thing I've found out since I came to live with Virgil and Bella is that you can never tell where *real* ends and *maybe* begins. You can do miracles with computers. It's called virtual reality. And yet there's always a tiny doubt in my mind. Is that *really* all it is – a computer miracle? Or is there something else – something more that no-one knows about except Virgil and Bella? Some reason why they are the only ones who can invent rides like *SPACE RANGER*, even though all the other theme parks in the country have got teams of scientists working to try and copy them? There's something Virgil and Bella can do that no-one else can. And it's the kind of secret people will do anything to get for themselves. I know that. That's why *they* are snooping round again. The Crowleighs.

We are lost in space. Will we ever get home? Earth is so small you can't even see it. Luckily Dinah is too little to be afraid of what's going to happen next. I'm afraid, always, every time I go on *SPACE RANGER*. What if I never get back, what if I'm lost out here in the darkness with the stars whirling around me? What if *SPACE RANGER* breaks down? I'll be in the middle of nothing, floating for ever, trying to find that tiny dot in the distance that means Earth and home.

But *SPACE RANGER* won't break down. Virgil and Bella would never let that happen. Everything's checked and checked and checked. The hot panic in me dies down as I feel our spacecraft start to swing. We're turning. We're going home.

When you climb down the steps from *SPACE RANGER*, you feel as if you've been away for a hundred years. But everything goes on just the same, as if you've only been away for a minute. We tumble out of the exit and there are crowds pushing round us, people shouting and babies screaming, ice creams melting on people's cornets.

'Let's get Zorro,' I say. We run back to the entrance and there he is, waiting for us with bright eyes. He whines with pleasure as I untie him, and licks my hand with his warm wet tongue.

'I want an ice cream,' says Dinah.

'Your mum should be here by now,' I say, looking around. Maybe Dinah's mum will buy us both ice creams . . . No chance, Nicky. She's not that sort of person. Dinah's mum should be here, but she isn't. Ten minutes, she said, and that was ages ago. And I haven't got any money for ice creams.

'There she is!' shouts Dinah, and points across to the café. A shiver of cold runs over me. There's Dinah's mum, sitting with her back to us at one of the tables in the café garden. And opposite her, leaning close, is a man in a heavy leather jacket with a scarf around his neck. He's wearing dark glasses so I can't see his eyes, but I know what they look like. They are cold and blue and they notice everything.

'Shh, Dinah! Don't shout!'

They haven't seen us yet. They're talking hard, heads close together.

'Why? Why can't I shout, Nicky? It's only Mum.'

'Wait a minute.'

I hold Dinah's hand tight so she won't run forward. If we stand really still, maybe he won't see us. He's taking something out of his pocket. A bit of paper. He's writing something on it. He pushes the paper across the table to Dinah's mum and she picks it up, puts it in her bag. The next minute he stands up and strides quickly away, towards *ANIMAL WORLD*. I let go of Dinah's hand.

'Mum! Mum!' yells Dinah, waving. Her mum hears her and swivels round on her chair. The next moment she's coming over to us.

'Dinah! Where've you been, you naughty girl? I was ever so worried about you.'

No, you weren't, I think. You were talking to *him*. But I smile and say nothing.

'I've been on *SPACE RANGER*!' shouts Dinah.

'Well, I hope it was worth hanging around for two hours, that's all I can say.'

'It was brilliant, wasn't it, Nicky? First of all we—'

'You can tell me about it later, dear. We're in a hurry. Say thank you to the little girl for looking after you so nicely.'

Little girl! Dinah's mum gives me a sugary smile. Now, why is she creeping round me like this, after she was so rude before? What's made her change?

Dinah puts her arms around Zorro's neck and hugs him hard.

'Oh, I wish we didn't have to go. I'll never see you again, Zorro.'

''Course you will,' says her mum sharply. 'Don't talk such nonsense, Dinah. After all, this is a nice place for a day out – and seeing as we live so close—' She flashes me another smile. 'And seeing as Nicky lives here.' There's something wrong with the way she says it. As if she likes me, but I know she doesn't really. She'd much rather snap at me, but for some reason she's switching on this smile instead. She reminds me of someone but I can't think who.

'See you then, Dinah,' I say.

'Which is your caravan, dear?' asks Dinah's mum. 'Just in case she can't find you another time.'

I point. 'Over behind those trees. The green and white one. That's our trailer.'

'Maybe Dinah could have a look round inside next time. That'd be a treat, wouldn't it, Diney?'

'I'd have to ask Virgil and Bella.'

'Virgil and Bella. Is that your mum and dad?'

'No,' I say. I'm not going to explain it all to *her*. It's bad enough at school. How does a nice kid like Dinah have such a horrible mother?

'See you then, Dinah,' I say. 'I've got to help Virgil and Bella now.'

Dinah's mum's eyes are still hungry with more questions, but I don't give her a chance. I smile at Dinah, give a wave which might include her mum, and walk away.

I'm halfway to our trailer when I realize who it is that Dinah's mum reminds me of. Smiling when she doesn't want to smile. Pretending to like me when she really hates me. She's just like Joe Marr.

Three

When I open the trailer door, a rich smell of chocolate floats out and wraps around me. It's the smell of birthdays and good times. It's the smell of the richest, stickiest, shiniest, most chocolate cake in the world. Virgil's chocolate cake. It takes hours to make. You have to grate the finest chocolate by hand and then stir it into the mixture very very slowly, while the mixing-bowl balances over a bowl of steaming water. If you do it wrong everything separates into gunge and you have to start again. And then the icing! The icing's fantastic. I can't make it foam into chocolate peaks the way Virgil can, but he lets me help, and I smoothe off the edges with a hot knife while he does the icing writing with white chocolate.

Virgil has his back to me and he's bent

over the kitchen table with the cake on an icing stand in front of him, one of those stands that twirls as you work.

'Hey, whose birthday is it? What's happening?'

'Come and look.'

He gives the stand one last twirl and the cake spins round, too fast for me to read at first. As it slows I see the words. *Thunder and Lightning*, it says, in Virgil's beautiful handwriting. There are fiery zigzags of white icing across the cake.

'What's it mean?' I ask.

'We have something to celebrate,' says Virgil. 'Wait till Bella comes.'

'And then you'll tell me?'

'Then we'll tell you.'

They do everything their own way, Virgil and Bella. I'm used to it now. They can keep a secret so well that I don't even guess it's there, then suddenly they'll tell me everything. I don't want to think about anything but the buzz of excitement. *Something to celebrate*. But a cold feeling nags at me. That man with the hard blue eyes and the leather jacket who talked to Dinah's mum. I know he means danger. Maybe there were more of *them* here today and I never noticed. Maybe in the hamburger queue – or down in the quietest part of the park, beyond the lake where there aren't any rides. Watching and waiting. I know they're looking for something. They want to get what we've got. You have to be careful in this business. *SPACE RANGER* is a magnet pulling in crowds for miles. Pulling them away from other theme parks, away from other people's rides. Pulling the money in, to us. And there're plenty of people who don't like that. That's why Virgil and Bella tell me never to say anything to anyone about our rides or what goes on in their locked workshop. I don't know that much, anyway.

But if I tell Virgil and Bella about the man now I'll spoil the celebration. And I don't want to do that. It's great when it's all of us together, with the cake in the middle of the table, and maybe steak and chips. And there'll be champagne. There's always champagne when Virgil and Bella celebrate. I always open it. I stand on the top step of our trailer and ease out the cork s-l-o-w-l-y the way Bella's shown me, and it pops and goes flying over the yellow, trampled-on grass. And then the champagne foams up and I splash it into the glasses. I get a small glass if we're having a party, but I like the look of it more than the taste. Dad always used to drink beer.

'Bella's gone shopping,' says Virgil. 'Gone to get a nice bit of steak. You hungry, Nicky?'

''Course I am.'

Virgil stares at his cake. 'Thunder and Lightning,' he says slowly, and there's a crackle of excitement in his voice, and I know this time it's something big. His gold cuff-links wink at me from the table. Real heavy gold, in the shape of anchors. Virgil's got his sleeves rolled up for baking, and he's wearing the kind of clothes no-one else but Virgil would ever wear in the kitchen. His black suit with long tails, that I last saw him wear to the grand opening of *SPACE RANGER*. And he's wearing a stiff white shirt with little pleats all across the front. There are a couple of dabs of icing-sugar on the front of his jacket, like a ghost's fingerprints.

'You've got stuff on your suit, Virgil.'

He glances down and shrugs. 'It'll come off,' he says. 'Pass me that other icing-bag, Nicky – the little one.'

'This one?'

'Yeah, that's it.' He bends down again, concentrating, and adds a sudden storm of raindrops around the lightning flashes. Then he straightens up and looks at me.

'You want to do some?'

I take the icing-bag and very carefully

squeeze out a couple of raindrops of white icing. Virgil's nice like that. He never wants to do every single little bit himself. I look up at him and smile. Then I notice that the front of his jacket is solidly, immaculately black. There isn't the ghost of a mark of icing-sugar on it any more.

The champagne bottle's empty. We've eaten the steak and chips, and all the chocolate cake except one wedge. I ate three slices, and as long as I keep still I feel OK. Bella's wearing her long, midnight-blue velvet dress, the one that reaches to her feet and has tiny stars sewn in all over it. Bella's clothes aren't like anyone else's. I don't know if I like them as clothes, but they look good on Bella. Diamonds flash from the band tying her hair back. Of course, they aren't real diamonds. They can't be. They'd cost thousands and thousands of pounds if they were real, they're so big. They flash blue and white fire as she turns her head and I can't stop staring at them. I've never seen them before. I wonder where Bella keeps them?

Bella catches me looking. 'You want to try them, Nicky?'

'No,' I say, but I do, and Bella knows it.

'Here, go on,' she says. She pushes back my

hair, and fastens the band round it. It's really heavy.

'Look at yourself,' she says. We've got a mirror propped over the sink, where Virgil shaves. I peer in. The diamonds flash on me just as they did on Bella. They don't look quite right though. There's too much of them. I look stupid staring out from under them.

'No, you don't,' says Bella. 'You're just not used to yourself.' I've given up wondering how Bella seems to know exactly what I'm thinking sometimes. Other times she doesn't even notice I'm there.

We've had the celebration but I still don't know what we're celebrating. I'm not going to ask, though. Let them tell me. I know they will, any minute now. And I'm right. Virgil lights a long thin cigar, pushes back his chair and smiles at Bella.

'We did it,' he says. They smile at each other, then, both at once as if they've agreed what to do, they turn and smile at me.

'We did it,' says Virgil again.

'We've done the next ride, Nicky,' says Bella, and her eyes flash as brightly as the diamonds.

'It's got to be good,' I think. Everyone's waiting to see what we're going to do next.

But the way they're smiling, I know it's OK. Virgil and Bella aren't stupid. They know it's going to be hard to follow *SPACE RANGER*. Everybody's waiting for them to get it wrong, so they can say the Damianos are past it. But they won't say that this time, I know it just by looking at Virgil and Bella. They look as if lights have been switched on inside them. Bella winks at Virgil and fixes the diamond band back in her hair with her quick fingers. She has long, clever fingers.

'Go on, then,' she says. 'You tell her.'

'She's seen the cake,' says Virgil. 'She knows what it's called, don't you, Nicky?'

'*THUNDER AND LIGHTNING*,' I say slowly. 'Yeah, but what's it all about? What kind of a ride is it?'

'You remember that night we were coming back over Salisbury Plain? When there was that storm?'

I nod. How could I ever forget it? I'd been half-asleep in the back of the van. We'd been fetching some stuff from Southampton – computer stuff Virgil and Bella needed. It had been shipped over from America. We had it in the back of the van all carefully crated up; so much of it, there was only enough room for me to curl up in the corner with my sleeping bag. It was late and dark and Virgil and

Bella's voices kept coming and going as I slid in and out of sleep. Then the storm started. There was a rush of wind that rocked the van, then a roar of rain. It was worse than being in a car wash. The windscreen wipers went faster and faster but they just sloshed the water from side to side without getting rid of it. Bella was driving and she slowed right down because she couldn't see. The van crawled forward while the wind sucked and howled and tried to push us off the road. Then everything turned blue. The lightning didn't just flash – it stayed on like a blue light with the switch jammed, a monster light that lit up everything. I peered forward past Bella's shoulder, through the torrents of rain, and into the weird, crackling, blue light. In that second I saw everything. The whole lit-up plain right to the horizon. And on the horizon there was a huge *something*. Or *someone*. Shoulders bent against the wind, huge pillars of legs. Miles away, but so big it couldn't be human. A *giant*. Then the light flicked off and there was a second of rushing rain.

'Bella!' I yelled. 'There's a—'

Then the thunder roared down on us. The van rattled and shook as if the noise was pulling it apart. Rain spouted down the windscreen. I couldn't tell if we were going forward or not. There was another huge flash of lightning and this time I saw Bella's face. She was looking at Virgil, and she was laughing.

'I saw a giant!' I screamed, but this time the thunder hit almost at the same second as the lightning.

'It's overhead!' Bella yelled. 'Right overhead!'

I didn't know she meant the storm. I thought she meant the giant, striding through the thunder and lightning to get us.

Of course, I don't believe in giants. Nobody believes in giants. Except in the middle of massive thunderstorms at midnight on Salisbury Plain, with the thunder and lightning pouncing on them like a cat on a mouse.

'It was Stonehenge,' said Bella much later, when the thunder was just a faraway rumble hidden in the swish of our tyres.

'What?'

'Stonehenge, Nicky. That giant you saw. It was the stones on the horizon. The lightning made it look different.'

But I'd seen huge shoulders, massive striding legs. I knew I had.

'It was the lightning,' said Bella.

'You'll never see a storm like that again,' said Virgil. 'Not so close.'

'Won't she?' said Bella. 'Won't she? I'm not so sure . . . ' Something like the lightning sizzled in her voice. She pushed back her hair with one hand and pressed her foot down on the accelerator. The van leaped forward and the road unrolled in front of us like wet liquorice. It was still raining but now it was just heavy rain falling straight down. Bella stared straight ahead. She was biting her lower lip the way she did when she was thinking hard. I thought she was concentrating on driving because the road was so wet. But she wasn't. *THUNDER AND LIGHTNING*. That's when they first thought of it.

'A storm,' says Virgil, leaning forward over the table.

'But not an ordinary storm,' says Bella. 'You start off in your car, like we were. But not a van, just an ordinary car so you can see out of all the windows.'

'You get strapped in,' says Virgil, 'just like you're going for a Sunday drive.'

'A bit boring, really,' says Bella. 'And off you go. Night-time, nothing happening. You can't see anything.'

'And just when you're thinking of asking for your money back—'

'It begins.'

'The storm.'

'Thunder—'

'And lightning.'

'Like we had?' I ask.

'Worse,' says Bella.

'Much worse,' says Virgil.

'You put out your hand, you can feel the lightning crackle over it,' says Bella.

'And the wind'll rock your car right up on two wheels.'

'The rain's coming in through the windscreen.'

'And the lightning's dancing on the bonnet.'

'But that's nothing.'

'No.'

They stop, and look at me expectantly.

'Like it so far?'

'Yeah!'

'You know the next bit.'

'No, I don't. Oh! You mean – the giant?'

'Of course. First of all you see him the way you did, Nicky. Miles away on the horizon. You blink because he can't be real. Then it goes dark and there's thunder. When the lightning comes again he's closer. Huge. Towering over the trees. Great legs striding over the plain.

Coming closer. And this time there's no doubt about it. He's real. And it goes dark.'

'What – what does he do then?'

'He picks up the car.'

'What! He can't! Giants aren't real!'

'Aren't they?' says Virgil.

'He picks up the car. He lifts it up high into the air and shakes it a little. You see his giant middle finger against the window on one side of the car, and his giant thumb on the other, pressed against the glass. He lifts the car with you in it, higher and higher until you're level with his face. You can see one eye coming closer and closer like a huge electric-blue lake with bristling reeds all round it. Below you there's the slope of his cheek and the slide of his nose which is so steep it makes you dizzy. He opens his mouth wider and wider and you see his red shiny gums and the yellow crags of his teeth and the long dark disappearing hole of his gullet and you're coming closer and closer—'

'And then,' says Virgil, 'you hear—'

'And then,' says Bella, 'you see—'

'What? What do you see? What do you hear?'

'Thunder,' says Virgil.

'Lightning,' says Bella.

‘That’s where the storm’s coming from,’ says Virgil.

‘Thunder from his mouth,’ says Bella.

‘And lightning from his eyes.’

‘Wow,’ I say. ‘You mean – they come out while he’s holding you? Thunder and lightning?’

‘Yes.’

‘Won’t people go deaf?’

‘We’ve done lots of tests,’ says Bella.

Won’t they die of fright? I want to say, but I don’t. They are both looking at me so expectantly.

‘Quite a simple idea,’ says Virgil. ‘But thanks to you, Nicky, an original one.’

Thanks to me! Wow. They’ve never said anything like that before.

‘It’s your giant, of course. Your Stonehenge giant. So we’re going to put your name on it. *Thunder and Lightning*, by Virgil, Bella and Nicky Damiano.’

For a long time I can’t say anything. I just repeat it over in my head. *‘By Virgil, Bella and Nicky. Thunder and Lightning, by Virgil, Bella and Nicky Damiano.’*

‘And you’ll have a percentage of the profits,’ adds Bella. ‘It’s about time you had some money of your own.’

I look down at the table. Instead of our cake

plates I see piles of five pound notes and tens and twenties, all counted out and sorted into bundles and sealed with white bands with a figure scribbled on them.

'Five per cent, we thought,' says Virgil.

And I look at their shiny smiling faces and know I'm going to get five per cent of something wonderful.

Four

I still haven't told Virgil and Bella. Why haven't I? Stupid! Really stupid! Just because I didn't want to take that shiny look off their faces. I kick a stone and it bounces under the trailer. Rain's mizzling down. And I've got to wash the mud off the trailer steps and then buy some bread and then . . . Boring. Why can't I be in the workshop?

Bella's at the *SPACE RANGER* pay booth today. Joe Marr didn't turn up to work this morning. We don't know why. So Bella's sitting there in her black and silver leggings and her silver T-shirt with a lightning flash of black down the back. Nobody mucks about when Bella's on the pay booth. Even really big kids just get their money out and say 'One for *SPACE RANGER*' in polite little voices. They muck about with Joe Marr even though he's so big and he's always grumpy and shouting. But Bella's different. Her eyes snap at you and she looks as if she could do anything.

I go to the standpipe and run off a bucketful of water. It's quite nice sloshing it over the steps. They are made of twisty iron in the shape of flowers, and the petals and leaves get full of mud where we walk up and down in our boots. I brush hard and more mud comes off. The steps look much better, but there's rain on my neck and everything feels flat after the champagne last night. Even Zorro's in a bad mood. He's crawled under the trailer to get out of the rain. It's all right for him. I hate it when Zorro won't do things with me.

Suddenly I hear someone shouting, 'Nicky! Nicky!' I turn round. It's Dinah flapping towards me in a slicker that's miles too big for her. Her mum's just behind. Dinah keeps on yelling 'Nicky!' even after I've waved back with the scrubbing brush. There's a big smile on her mum's face, and she speaks to me in the sugary voice again.

'I hope you don't mind. Dinah went on and on about coming to see you.'

'Oh – that's OK.'

'You said I could come, Mum. What're you doing, Nicky?'

'Washing the steps, what does it look like?'

Her mum breaks in again. 'Nicky, can Dinah stay with you for a bit? I've got to meet my friend and she'll just get bored. She wants to play with your dog.'

I think Dinah's mum is a bit cheeky, but I don't say anything. Dinah looks so hopeful.

'All right.'

Dinah's mum fusses round for a bit, fixing up a time for us to meet her at the ice-cream booth, but I can tell she can't wait to go. As soon as she's down the steps and across the grass, Dinah bursts out:

'Guess what, Nicky! My brother's here.'

She says 'my brother' in that way little kids do, as if he's really special.

'Oh,' I say scratchily. 'Well, I've got to finish this.'

'Don't you want to see him?'

'Mm, yeah. Only not just now. I'm busy.'

'But he can't come out.'

'How can he be here if he can't come out? Mind your feet,' and I slosh a stream of muddy water away down the steps.

'Mum brought him in the car. But he's not allowed out in the rain in case he gets cold. He's waiting for us in the café.'

Suddenly I remember. 'I thought he was in hospital.'

'They let him out this morning. Mum and I fetched him.'

'He should be in bed, then, shouldn't he, if he's just got out of hospital?'

Dinah shakes her head. 'He's always going to hospital. He has his keemo there.'

'Keemo? What's that?'

'It's medicine that helps his blood.'

'Oh, I see.' I don't, but it's a bit annoying when little kids use words you don't understand.

'You've got to come, Nicky! I told him about you.'

The steps are as clean as they're ever going to get. I empty the bucket. 'I've got to go and buy some bread.'

'Oh.'

She sounds really disappointed. She's staring down at the muddy water seeping into the ground. She won't look at me.

'Oh, all right then. I'll come. I can get the bread after.'

Dinah looks up and her face curls into a big smile. 'Can you bring Zorro? I told Steve about Zorro.'

'Not in the café. He's not allowed.'

'Oh.'

That little sad *Oh*. It shouldn't work but it does.

'All right, then. I'll bring Zorro and he can sit just outside the door so Steve can see him out of the window. It's dry there.'

Zorro doesn't want to come out from under the trailer, but I say, 'Bones, Zorro!' and get one from the trailer for him to eat while we're in the café. Then he can't come fast enough. He remembers Dinah and lets her hug him though all the time he keeps watching the bag with his bone in it.

'All right, Zorro, you'll get it!'

I see Steve before he sees us. He's sitting at a window table. The windows are steamed up because of the rain but he's rubbed a clear patch and he's staring out at the rain. He looks tired and pale. Perhaps he doesn't really want to be here. Perhaps it was all Dinah's idea.

'Dinah,' I say casually, 'do you know who your mum's friend is, the one she's going to meet?'

'Oh, it's just the friend we saw when we were here before,' says Dinah.

A friend who wears a leather jacket and dark glasses even when the sun's not shining. A friend who hangs around, watching and waiting, noticing everything. A friend who's after something. I really wish I'd said something to Bella and Virgil. I kneel down by Zorro and tie his lead to the hook in the café wall.

'Listen, I won't be long. Here's your bone.'

Steve's my age. His face through the café window looked older somehow. I sit down a bit shyly and smile at him. We both start speaking at once.

'Dinah's told me—'

'Dinah's told me—' Then we both stop and laugh. He's drinking a banana milkshake and I say I'll get milkshakes for Dinah and me.

'I'll pay for Dinah's,' says Steve. 'Mum gave me some money.'

'Oh, it's OK, I've got loads of money,' I say. It's not quite true, but it soon will be, once I start getting my five per cent of the takings from *THUNDER AND LIGHTNING*.

I bring the milkshakes back to our table. Steve's watching Zorro outside, eating his bone.

'Is he yours? He's fantastic.'

'Yeah, he's mine. Well, mostly mine. Want to come out and have a look afterwards?'

But Steve hesitates. 'I'm not really supposed to.'

I look at him. 'Only for a minute! That won't hurt, will it? Anyway, your mum's not here.'

Steve flushes. It makes me realize how pale he was before. 'It's not that. It's got nothing to do with Mum. It's the chemo. It makes me catch cold and stuff really easily.'

That word again. But as I look at Steve, even though I don't understand what it means, I start to understand something. He's so pale. And his hair must be really short because it's all under his baseball cap – in fact I can't see any hair at all—

'It fell out because of the chemo,' says Steve. 'That's what you want to ask, isn't it? That's what everyone wants to ask.'

'Oh. No. I wasn't going to—' I feel my own face go fiery red. But suddenly Steve grins.

''Course you were. Don't worry, I'm used to it.'

I grin back, relieved.

'Nicky!' hisses Dinah, digging me hard in the side with her elbow.

'What?'

'That man. He's looking at us again. Do you think he's a stranger?'

I look where she's looking. No leather jacket today, but he's still wearing the dark glasses. He's got a newspaper on the table in front of him but I don't think he's reading it. I can't see his eyes at all through those glasses but I know just what they look like. And I know for sure now that he's one of *them*. A Crowleigh. Dinah's mum's friend. So where's Dinah's mum? I bet she's still looking for him.

'He *is* a stranger, isn't he?' whispers Dinah.

'He's strange, all right. But don't let him see you looking.'

We all lean forward and suck our straws.

'What's going on?' asks Steve.

'Oh – I'm not sure. It's probably nothing.'

'No, it's not. I can tell it's not from the way you're looking.'

'You get funny people hanging round theme parks sometimes,' I say.

'Is that why you've got Zorro? To chase them away?' asks Dinah.

'Yeah. Sort of.'

'Watch out. He's coming over here,' says Steve.

And he is. The café furniture looks little and flimsy as he pushes his way through it, over to our table. Chairs grate back and the little jar of flowers on the next table shivers. Suddenly I realize there's no-one else in the café. Behind the counter, Rosie's got her back to us as she wipes down one of the urns.

He stands looking down at us, tapping his rolled-up paper against his leg. Now he's so close I can see his eyes even through the dark glasses, and I wish I couldn't. They take us all in, coldly, thoroughly, missing nothing. I feel their cold spreading deep inside me.

'That your dog outside?' he asks. If anyone was listening they'd think it was an ordinary question. They'd think he just liked dogs.

'Yeah,' I say.

'What's that he's eating?'

'A bone.'

'Oh. A bone. Where's he got that from, I wonder?'

'I gave it him,' I say as rudely as I dare.

'Oh, you did, did you? That's lucky, 'cos they pick up all kinds of stuff, dogs do. You never know where it's been. And some of it's quite – nasty. We wouldn't want your dog eating anything like that, would we? Zorro, isn't it?'

'How do you know his name?' asks Dinah.

''Course I know his name. I like dogs. And they like me. They'll do anything for me, dogs will.'

He smiles. A big smile that stretches his face without making it look any friendlier. And he puts up a hand and takes off his dark glasses. His blue eyes stare over my head at Zorro gnawing his bone.

'Bet he's a greedy dog. Bet he'll eat anything. Am I right or am I right? Bet he hasn't learned to keep his mouth shut. Any more than you have. So you'd better learn, hadn't you? Or else it might be too late for Zorro.'

We say nothing. The café is frozen. Then suddenly, behind me, I see Rosie turn. She looks over at us, looks again, frowns. As quick as lightning the man glances round, smiles, pats Dinah's head and walks out of the café. He doesn't seem to hurry but he's gone in a second. Rosie flaps her dishcloth at me. 'You OK, Nicky? For a minute I thought there was something funny going on.'

'We're OK. Thanks, Rosie.'

'He's horrible!' bursts out Dinah. 'He's really horrible.'

'Yeah. We know. You don't have to tell us,' says Steve.

I can hardly get the words out. 'Do you think he was trying to say – he was going to do something to Zorro?'

'Yeah,' says Steve. 'Yeah, I think he was. You should watch him.'

'He's really horrible!' says Dinah again. 'Why does Mum like him?'

'Mum! What's Mum got to do with it?' Steve sounds angry.

'He's Mum's friend. Isn't he, Nicky?'

'I don't know.'

'Yes, he is. I know he is. They were talking.'

'Well. Maybe,' I say cautiously, watching Steve.

'It's a load of rubbish, Dinah,' says Steve. 'Mum wouldn't be friends with *him*.'

I think of how their mum and the man sat together talking, leaning forward, as if it was something really important. I don't like their mum but I can't believe she's really one of *them*. Maybe she's being blackmailed. Maybe they've promised her something if she does what they say. But I can't tell Steve that.

'You're really stupid, Dinah, if you think Mum would have anything to do with him,' says Steve confidently. Dinah sucks her straw and gives him a long look, but says nothing.

'Does Zorro sleep in your trailer?' Steve asks me.

'No. He sleeps outside.'

'Maybe you ought to bring him in.'

'But he's a guard dog. No-one would dare touch him. He's really fierce with strangers.'

'But what if they give him a bone or something – or some meat?'

All the warmth drains out of me. Zorro. They can't hurt Zorro. Every single day since I've been here, Zorro's been with me. Ever since Dad—

I get up quickly, knocking back my chair.

'Where are you going?'

'I've got to make sure Zorro's OK.'

''Course he is. Look, I can see him from here,' says Steve.

'I know, but—' I keep moving towards the door.

'Come back afterwards then, OK?' Steve calls after me.

'OK.'

The air is cool on my face after the steamy café. Zorro's lying with his head on his paws, but as soon as he sees me he gets up and growls a welcome deep in his throat. I put out my hand and he closes his mouth on it so gently his lips feel like warm velvet.

'All right, boy? You all right, Zorro?'

He growls again, tickling my fingers. ''Course you are. No-one's going to hurt you, boy. Not ever. I won't let them—'

But I know it's not as easy as that. Bad things happen, and sometimes you can't stop them. I think of Dad. It was just before Christmas, the last time he went into hospital. Only of course then I didn't know it was the last time. That was after Dad had written to Virgil and Bella, and Bella had come to stay with me in our flat. That was nice. I'd been staying at my friends' houses so long that it was good to be in my own room again. I've always really, really loved Christmas. Dad and I used to make all our own decorations. We didn't just have one tree, we had three. One in the living-room, one in my bedroom, and one in the back yard. Our yard was tiny, but it looked beautiful with the lights lit on the tree at night and the big gold star Dad made glittering on top. In my room I had a tiny tree with gold moons and stars I'd made myself out of Fimo, and then painted. I wound tinsel all round it, and there was a huge mobile of silver angels flying over it. And Dad fixed up some tree lights for me too, that last year, just before he went back into hospital. I was eight. A year older than Dinah. I'd bought Dad a big chocolate Father Christmas wrapped in red and gold paper and put loads of ribbon round it, and a pair of bedsocks because his feet were always cold now, and I'd made him a card.

About ten days before Christmas I got home from school early. My school was really close and I had a key in a special bag that went round my waist. I opened the door and it was all dark. I thought Bella must be down at the shop. I switched on the lights and went to look at my tree. Then I thought I'd do something special for Dad. I knew that hospitals always tried to let people come home for Christmas. I had some red foil card left from making my decorations, and a big piece of card which was

Dad's but he wasn't using it. I started drawing letters and cutting them out and sticking them onto the card. It was a poster for Dad. I wasn't all that good at spelling then, but I can remember what it said. WELCOME HOME, DAD. I stuck all the letters on and sprayed some silver glitter all over the card. It looked fantastic. Then I heard the key in the lock. I jumped a bit, but it was only Bella.

'Oh. Nicky. Hi, I'm sorry I'm late. I had to go to the hospital.'

She flopped down on a chair and kicked off her boots. Then she said, 'What're you doing?'

'Making something.'

'Can I see?'

Slowly I turned the poster round. Bella looked at it for a long time. I thought she was cross with me for using all the stuff, even though Dad let me, so I said, 'It's my foil and spray and everything,' but she only said, 'It's beautiful. He'd love to see it. I think we should go there right now, Nicky, and take it to show him.'

'But,' I started, 'it's for when he comes home—'

'I know. Look, it rolls up, doesn't it? It would be great in your dad's room in the hospital.'

I stared at her. Dad wasn't in a room, he was in a long ward with lots of other people.

'They've moved your dad into a special room of his own,' said Bella. 'So it's quieter for him. He's very tired, Nicky. Very tired.'

The way she said it I knew she was telling me something else. Something much bigger hid under her words.

'But if I take it to the hospital, then he won't have a poster when he comes home.'

She didn't say anything. She didn't say, *That's all right, you can make another one*. She just looked at me, rolled up the poster, found an elastic band and snapped it round. Then she held out her hand and said, 'Come on, Nicky. Let's go.'

But I ran back into my bedroom. It was dark but all the lights on my Christmas tree were on, warm and friendly and a bit mysterious, the way Christmas trees look at night. The big silver angels drifted round and round on the mobile Dad had helped me to make. Each angel had a long silver trumpet. The tree was alive, growing in a big pot full of earth. After Christmas we were going to put it out in the yard, so it could grow all year and then it could come into my room again next Christmas. I remembered Dad saying, 'Don't forget to water your tree while I'm away, Nicky. Otherwise it'll die and you won't be able to use it next year.'

Under the tree there were his presents and his card. *To Dad, with loads and loads of love from Nicky. Happy Christmas!* I picked them up. Bella had come to my door and was standing there looking at me.

'I'm going to take Dad's Christmas present in to the hospital for him,' I said. I waited. Maybe – maybe Bella would say, *'Don't be silly, Nicky. It's not Christmas yet.'* But she didn't. Instead she smiled and said, 'That's a good idea, Nicky. He'll like that.'

I looked at my Christmas tree with the red and green and gold lights winking in its branches. I'd remembered to water it, so it wasn't going to die. I could have it again next year if I wanted.

Then I bent down and switched off the lights.

My head is against Zorro's and his soft fur rubs my face. I want to stay here for ever, never go back into the café, never have to talk to Steve and Dinah about that man and the bad things he's trying to do to us, never get worried or frightened again. Zorro's thick black fur is warm and safe. Safe. No. Zorro isn't safe. Not unless I do something. Now.

I get up. My jeans are muddy from kneeling on the ground by Zorro. 'Back soon, boy! Stay!'

Five

'You don't want to tell me, do you?' says Steve.

'It's not that. I do, but—'

'But?'

'Well—'

'It's my mum, isn't it? It's what Dinah said. You think she's friends with *him*. You think I'll tell her and then she'll go off and tell him everything. Is that it?'

'I'm sorry, Steve. But you don't really understand what it's like here. You're a Daisy—'

As soon as I've said it I wish I hadn't.

'Daisy? What's that? What d'you mean?'

'Well, a Daisy is – like – a visitor. They just come for the day. All the people who come to Mere Park are Daisies. They just go on the rides. They don't know what's behind any of it.'

'Oh,' says Steve. He pulls his baseball cap

down a bit more. 'So we can't be friends, is that what you mean?'

'I don't know.'

'But you must have friends outside here. What about school?'

'I don't go to school.'

'*Don't go to school!* Wow! Isn't that against the law?'

'Well – I have lessons. Sort of. Bella and Virgil teach me things. And I work with the computers. Then I do the money and I help write adverts. That's Maths and English.'

'Doesn't anyone make you go?'

'No, I—'

I don't want to talk about it. I don't want to talk about the kids at the school I went to when I first came here. They didn't like people who live in trailers. Their parents told them things about us. They didn't like Virgil and Bella. There was lots of whispering all the time, and when I came close it would stop and they'd look at me and laugh. Then they found out about Dad and there was this boy who kept on asking about it.

'What did you say your dad died of? Hey! Her dad died of a virus! What's a virus, Miss?' Then more whispering. '*My mum says . . . my dad told me . . .* ' I never said anything. They started calling me Dumbo Damiano.

'It's a bit like me,' says Steve quickly. 'I don't go to school a lot either. I have a teacher in hospital who comes round.' He smiles. 'I don't reckon we're missing much, do you?'

He's nice. He's really nice. I smile.

'I wouldn't say anything to Mum, you know,' he says. Both at the same time, we glance at Dinah.

'Dinah—'

'I won't say anything! I promise!'

'Not even by mistake when you're thinking about something else? It means being really careful.'

'I will be, Steve. I'll be really careful. Steve, can I go to the toilet?'

'Yeah, but don't be too long.'

She skips off, threading her way between the tables. She looks really happy. I hope none of that whispering stuff at school ever happens to Dinah. I turn back to Steve.

'All right, then,' I say. 'You know *SPACE RANGER*?'

'Mm, 'course I do.'

'You know it's made loads of money? It's been on TV and everything?'

'Yeah. I saw it on the news when I was in hospital.'

I glance round to make sure no-one's listening. There's a woman with a baby two tables away, but she's got her back to us. She's busy stopping the baby grabbing her sandwich. I lean forward again. 'We're developing the next ride. The one that's going to follow *SPACE RANGER*.'

'But everyone says *SPACE RANGER* is fantastic. Why don't you just keep it?'

I sigh. He really is a Daisy after all. 'You can't do that. You've got to keep one step ahead. Give people what they want before they know they want it. Otherwise they get bored and they go somewhere else.'

'Oh, I see. Yeah, I suppose you're right,' says Steve slowly. 'So what's the new ride?'

'I can't tell you. I can't tell anyone. But it's really good. Even better than *SPACE RANGER*. And I think people have guessed we're doing it. They're getting jealous. They're trying to find out about the new ride.'

'Because you'll get all the customers,' says Steve.

'That's right. And I think I know who's trying to find out.'

'Who?'

'Swear you won't say. Not to anyone. 'Specially not—'

'My mum. I know. I'm not stupid. Only you're wrong about her.'

'OK, OK.' I pretend to duck. Steve smiles, but he's looking very white, as if he ought to be at home, in bed.

'You all right, Steve?'

'Just tired.'

'They're called the Crowleighs. There are loads of them. They used to be a circus family, like the Damianos, only there aren't so many circuses now. People don't like going to see the performing animals any more. Virgil and Bella got into computer rides before anyone else did. Long before the Crowleighs thought of it. Now we've got virtual reality and laser technology and everything. The Crowleighs are catching up but they've never invented a ride that's done as well as any of ours. Before *SPACE RANGER* opened, they were trying everything. Hacking into our computer system, even putting notes on the bulletin board of the Internet, trying to get information about us. Virgil and Bella slept in the workshop every night till *SPACE RANGER* opened, in case there was a break-in. The Crowleighs thought they could copy what we were doing, even though they never could in a million years. But no-one ever guessed *SPACE RANGER* would do as well as this. We've had huge traffic jams of Daisies all summer. The

Crowleighs say we're taking their customers.'

'Well, you are, aren't you?'

'Yeah, I suppose so. But that's life, isn't it?'

Steve looks at me. 'You sounded really hard when you said that, Nicky.'

I shrug. 'It's true.' This conversation isn't going quite the way I want. I want Steve to be on my side straight away, against the Crowleighs. But he's not.

'That man – the one who came up to us. He was a Crowleigh.'

'How d'you know?'

'His eyes. Those blue eyes. All the Crowleighs have them. Besides, I've seen him before.'

'And he knew you.'

'Yeah. That's why he said that stuff about Zorro.' Automatically, I glance sideways through the window and check that Zorro's still there, safe, dozing over his bone.

Steve looks awful. Perhaps I ought to ask him and Dinah to our trailer so he can lie down . . . *Dinah*.

'Steve. Dinah's not back.'

'Oh, she's always doing this. It's such a pain. She mucks about with the soap then she wets her hair and turns the hand dryer into a hair dryer. It drives Mum mad.'

'I'd better go and get her. You can come and have a look at our trailer, if it's not too far for you. It's stopped raining.'

'There's nothing wrong with my legs! I get tired, that's all. It's the chemo.'

'Right, I'll just get Dinah and we'll go.'

But there's no Dinah splashing at the basins. No Dinah mucking about at the hair dryers. One of the toilet cubicles is open and empty. The other two are closed.

'Dinah! Dinah, come on out. We've been waiting ages for you.'

No answer. I push the first door. It isn't locked and it swings open easily, showing another empty cubicle. Suddenly I am afraid to push open the last door.

'Dinah!' My voice echoes a bit then disappears in the silence. I push the last door but I already know what I'll see. An empty cubicle. I bang the door shut and rush out of the toilets. Where is she?

'Steve! She's not in there! Did you see her go out?'

'Are you sure? Did you look properly?'

''Course I'm sure! Look yourself if you want to.'

'She can't have gone out. We'd have seen her – wouldn't we?'

'Yeah . . .' But I'm not so sure. We were

leaning forward, not thinking about anything except the rides and the Crowleighs.

I look across the café. Rosie is flipping toasties out of the sandwich-maker for a family standing by the counter. The woman with the baby has gone.

'I'll ask Rosie.'

Steve comes with me. 'I shouldn't have let her go on her own. Mum'll go mad—'

'She'll be round here somewhere. She'll be mucking about, you said so yourself.'

'Yeah. I hope so.'

We wait till Rosie's finished with the customers.

'Rosie. You know the little girl who was with us? Did she go out?'

'Oh yeah, that's right,' says Rosie. 'I meant to tell you. She went off with her mum. She left a message for you. She said, *"Tell the little Damiano girl I've taken Dinah."*'

'Didn't she leave a message for me?' asks Steve. We look at each other, relieved but still a bit puzzled. Why didn't his mum come over and tell us she was taking Dinah?

'No, just what I said,' says Rosie. 'She was busy with the baby.'

'Baby?' we both ask at once.

Rosie laughs. 'Go on, what's wrong with you? Didn't you see she had the baby with her? They were sitting right by you. Hasn't she got lovely blue eyes, your baby sister?' she goes on to Steve. 'Just like your mum's.'

'But—' Steve begins.

I tread on his foot. 'Oh, right. We'll see them later then. Thanks a lot, Rosie,' I gabble. I pull hard on the sleeve of Steve's jacket. 'Come *on*, Steve!'

'But—'

By now I've got him far enough away from Rosie to hiss, 'Don't say it! Keep quiet till we get outside.'

The sky's clearing and there is sun on the puddles. Zorro jumps up when he sees us come through the café door.

'But,' says Steve for the third time, 'Mum's got brown eyes.'

'I know that. You didn't think it was your mum, did you? It was the woman with the baby. I didn't see her eyes because she had her back to us.'

'You mean – she's one of *them*?'

I nod, untying Zorro. 'Yeah. She's a Crowleigh for sure. And the baby.'

'They've got Dinah, Nicky! They've got Dinah. What're we going to do?'

'Go to the trailer. Find Virgil and Bella. Tell them the Crowleighs are here. Come on.'

'We'll have to get the police.'

'No. Not the police. Not if you want to get Dinah back quick. Listen, Steve, we'll be quicker if we go after her ourselves.'

'Mum. What about Mum? I can't tell Mum, Nicky. She's had an awful time with me being ill. She'll go mad if she thinks something's happened to Dinah as well.'

'She'll never know. We're going to get Dinah back right now. The Crowleighs won't hurt her, it's me and Bella and Virgil they want to hurt, not Dinah. I can't work out why they've taken her. There must be a reason. What was that message?'

'Tell the little Damiano girl I've taken Dinah.'

'I can't work it out, can you?'

'What d'you mean, work it out? We've got to do something, Nicky! They've taken Dinah. And if they're like you said—'

'She wanted me to know. *Tell the little Damiano girl.* She wanted us all to know. She could have just taken Dinah and said nothing if she'd wanted.'

We are at the trailer. Steve holds the hand-rail tight as he climbs the steps. His legs look as if they're going to stop working soon. I unlock the door and push past him. 'Here. This is where I sleep. You can lie down.' My cabin is tiny. There's just about room for me to stand while Steve lets himself down onto my bunk and lies still, so still and white that for a moment I'm frightened. After all he's only just got out of hospital—

'Steve!'

He opens his eyes a bit. ''S OK. I'm just tired . . .'

'I'll get you a drink—'

'No. Dinah . . .'

But I get the drink first. Tea out of the big flask Virgil makes every morning and leaves on the table for anyone who wants some. Two spoons of sugar.

'Here, drink a bit of this.'

Steve half sits up and swallows some tea. He's looking a bit better, I think.

'That message,' I say. 'Why did she tell me she'd taken Dinah? She wanted me to know. Why?'

'Because she wanted – something – a ransom?'

'No. She doesn't even know if you've got any money. Something else.'

'She left the message for you, not me. She must have wanted you to do something.'

'Yes, that's it. I'm sure that's it.'

'Or,' says Steve, pulling himself to sit upright, 'not to do something.'

'What do you mean?'

'If we were looking for Dinah, then we couldn't be doing something else, could we?'

'Oh. Oh yes, I see. You're right. *If we were looking for Dinah we couldn't be doing anything else.* So that means—'

'We'd be out of the way.'

'Whatever they were doing, we wouldn't know about it. We wouldn't be able to stop it. Steve! I've got to find Virgil and Bella right away!'

'But what about Dinah?'

'We'll find Dinah,' I say, trying to sound sure even though I've no idea how we're going to find her. 'You stay here. I won't be long. Will you be all right?'

'Yeah,' he says, but he doesn't look so good. He doesn't look as if he ought to be left on his own.

'Listen, Steve. What if I leave Zorro with you? He'll look after you.'

Steve smiles. He reaches out his hand and rubs the soft fur under Zorro's chin. Most people are frightened of Zorro, but not Steve.

'That'd be great.'

'You look after Steve, Zorro. Stay!' Zorro gives me a look as if to say, *Do you think I'm stupid? I know what to do.*

I glance back from the door. Steve's eyes are shut again, but he's still stroking Zorro. It's nice having Zorro close when you feel bad. I'd better not lock the trailer, in case Steve wants to go out. I've got to look for Virgil and Bella – but where are they?

It feels funny not having Zorro with me. As if part of me missing.

Six

Where first? The workshop? Our computer control room? No, they won't be there. Everything's programmed. Usually Bella or Virgil goes in each morning to check and set up, and then the computer runs itself. Unless there's a problem and then the computer bleeps a message to the trailer. There's a back-up computer too – it's a really safe system.

They won't be on the video scanner. Mack's there all day. He even eats his sandwiches in there. He works for us, and his job is to operate the video scanner for *SPACE RANGER*, checking for problems. A lost kid, a fight, a queue that's getting too long. If he sees anything going wrong, he phones Virgil or Bella. I'm beginning to feel calmer. The Crowleighs can't do anything, not really. We've got all these safety checks and back-ups and we've got the scanner. And of course they won't hurt Dinah.

I'll go to the pay booth first. Unless Joe's come, Bella will still be there. But I won't be able to tell her with all those Daisies coming through buying their tickets. What about going to the workshop? Virgil might be in there.

To get to the workshop you have to go through the computer control room. You have to punch in a code to open the main door to the building first. The code changes all the time. I know it, I know I know it. 77. Yes. Something lucky. And then something unlucky. 13? No, it wasn't 13. Too obvious. 92. 92, that's it. The year Bella broke her leg. I punch in the numbers and the outer door swings open.

The fans hum. It's cool and shadowy, always the same temperature in here. The monitors wink, showing brightly coloured slews of numbers. But there's no-one here.

'Virgil?' He might be out the back. 'Virgil?' But no-one answers. There's only the fans, and the click of the computers saving. Suddenly one of the printers starts up. They print out a ride every hour, so it can be checked. I can't understand the printouts unless Virgil or Bella goes through one with me; all the figures relate to the different stages of the ride – velocity, speed, braking, drag and all those things. Then there's another printout to match the speed of the ride to the virtual reality sequence. It has to be a perfect match. They measure it down to hundredths of a second.

The printout starts snaking out of the printer. I'm watching it, so it's only by chance that I see something flicker on the screen nearest me. I just see it out of the corner of my eye, but for some reason it grabs my attention. It's not like a normal flicker. More a wobble, as if a column of figures has turned to jelly for a second. But when I look straight at the screen I can't see anything different from normal. I know which part of the program this is. It's where *SPACE RANGER* turns and heads for home. That bit where you're lost in space and you look out of the windows and you can't even see Earth. Just a thick forest of stars and blackness. It's frightening. Even though you know it's not real, even though you know for sure you're coming back, it's still frightening. And then *SPACE RANGER* begins to swing and you know you're going home. But I'm always glad that moment of fear doesn't last more than half a minute.

It doesn't last more than half a minute because Virgil and Bella have planned everything to the last second. Twenty-seven point four seconds precisely. They spend ages working out where the border is between fear that you half-enjoy and fear that leaves you sweating and trembling. OK, we have all the notices about people with heart conditions and people with nervous dispositions not going on them, but we're not trying to frighten anybody to death.

As I stare, it comes again. A wobble in the figures, as if a big hand I can't see is crushing them together, making pulp out of numbers. Then they straighten out and swim on down the screen again.

Something's wrong. It's never done this before. What's going on?

The wobble comes again, and this time it lasts longer. I hold my breath. Are the figures going to get back into shape or has the hand squeezed the life out of them?

Just in time, they straighten. They are normal.

Just in time. Because this isn't the computer that records how *SPACE RANGER* is running. It is the computer that programs the ride.

The figures shiver again, as if someone is tweaking them. But there's no-one in the control room except me. No-one at the keyboard.

I realize I'm still holding my breath. I let it out in a long shaky sigh. Don't be stupid, Nicky. It's all right. This computer has a built-in alarm system. If anything serious goes wrong, it'll bleep a message to Mack. There's an alarm icon on the right hand of the screen. Virgil showed me once how it flashes. But it's not flashing now. What's happened to it? Cautiously, I move my hand towards the mouse. I know how to check the alarm function because I've seen Virgil do it. It has to be done regularly. But Virgil and Bella have told me a million times never to touch this computer, because it's the programming computer.

But what if something's wrong? And they don't know? I'm only going to check the alarm function, I won't touch anything else. That can't possibly do any harm. Slowly, slowly, I slide my hand over the mouse. It feels like picking up a box of matches when I was a little kid and I wasn't allowed to touch them. I click the function box, run the arrow down the control options and click the one I want. A box flashes up on screen.

ALARM FUNCTION DISABLED

I can't believe it. I cancel and click again.

The same message flashes. I've never seen it before. I don't know how to un-disable it. I'll try the information box. I know how that works, too. There are so many options in the information box that it makes me feel dizzy when I scroll them. This one. **INFORMATION ON MALFUNCTION**. Then there's a long list of zones where the malfunction could be. I click **ALARM.**

ALARM FUNCTION DISABLED

it parrots back at me. I scroll again. Maybe there's something else that'll help. I click **LOCATE MALFUNCTION**. A bigger box flashes up on the left hand of the screen. There are five words in it, five words I've never seen before on any screen in this workshop.

A FATAL ERROR HAS OCCURRED

I stare at the screen. My hands are sweating. The mouse slips. What's going on? The computer blinks calmly back at me. It's not getting upset. It's just telling me what's happened.

No-one knows except me. If Virgil or Bella had seen that message they'd be right here in a minute, going through the program, finding the error. If Mack had been bleeped he'd be here. Whoever has been in this computer doesn't want anyone to know. That's why the alarm function was disabled. It's only by chance that there's anyone here at all to see what's happening. If we'd gone off looking for Dinah—

Tell the little Damiano girl I've taken Dinah.

That's what they wanted. Me looking for Dinah, rushing off to tell everyone she was missing. All the security people going into action. Mack turning the video scanner towards the exits, and to anywhere she might be hidden.

But we haven't told anyone. I'm here. And they don't know that. I wish I could understand the figures. I wish I could understand what they're doing to the program.

I go to the phone. I dial 52 first. That's the pay booth number. A voice answers: 'Pay booth here. *SPACE RANGER.*' It's Joe Marr. He must have come in after all. 'Pay booth here. *SPACE RANGER,*' he snaps again. Quietly, I put down the receiver. Let him think it's a wrong number.

The workshop. That's 66. It rings and rings but there's no answer. I let it keep ringing. After twenty rings it will switch on the answerphone automatically. Virgil's voice comes on. *'If you'd like to leave a message, please do so after the beep.'* It's so frustrating, hearing his voice and not being able to talk to him. But I leave a message: *'Virgil, it's me, Nicky. I've got to talk to you. Something's happened. I'm in the computer control room so can you ring me?'*

As soon as I finish the message I realize how stupid it is. I can't hang around here waiting for him to ring back. There's Steve in the trailer – and Dinah. We've to find Dinah.

The numbers bubble up on the computer screen. They are coming loose, away from the anchor of the program Bella and Virgil have developed so carefully, second by second so that it's fantastic and brilliant and exciting and terrifying – but safe. I feel a horrible chill, as if someone's standing right behind me, reaching forward to put their hands on the controls.

There's no-one there. But I realize in a flash that there doesn't need to be anyone there. That's the thing about computers. Someone's got into our program, someone who shouldn't be there. It's like a hand feeling around inside my head, trying to rearrange my brain. Is it the Crowleighs? I can't believe they've done it at last. Virgil and Bella always say they'll never to able to keep up with the technology we've got. Our software is the most advanced in any theme park ride in the world. That's why everyone wants it.

But I know it's much easier to muck things up than to make them. Think of how you make a really beautiful model and then someone smashes their foot down on it. By mistake or not, it doesn't matter. So many hours to build, so hard to make, and so easy to destroy. Lots of things are like that. The Crowleighs haven't got the technology to create anything like *SPACE RANGER*, but they might just know enough to destroy it. And this isn't happening by mistake. Someone's in our computer program, trying to change it, trying to damage it so it won't work. So that *SPACE RANGER* won't work.

Think, Nicky, think. You don't know where Virgil is. Bella was at the pay booth but she's not now. Joe Marr's no good. I'm almost sure he's in with *them*. *Mack*. I'll talk to Mack. He's got the video scanner. He might know what to do. He might know what's happened to Virgil and Bella. I'll get Steve and Zorro, then we'll find Mack. Steve'll be better now he's had a rest.

Suddenly I see the queue for *SPACE RANGER* clearly in my mind, as clearly as if it was on the computer screen in front of me. There are loads of Daisies waiting for their ride. They're paying their money and pushing forward, all excited because they can't wait to go on *SPACE RANGER*. They've been hearing about it for weeks, they've been queuing for nearly two hours, and now they're at the front. They're going to have a fantastic experience, they know that. I see the queue of Daisies in my mind and I shiver. It's not just *SPACE RANGER* that's in danger now the computer program isn't functioning properly. It's the Daisies, too. Daisies like Steve and Dinah. People. I need Virgil and Bella, but they're not here. I've got Zorro and Steve and maybe Mack. Four of us. That's not much. What can we do?

Seven

The heavy outer door of the computer control room slams shut behind me. Where first? Mack. The video scanner room. He'll be there for sure.

No. I've got to get Steve. I'm not sure Mack'll believe me if I rush in on my own and tell him about Dinah being kidnapped, the Crowleighs plotting to destroy *SPACE RANGER*, what's happening to the computer and all the rest of it. It sounds pretty unbelievable, even for the Crowleighs. But if there are two of us, Mack will have to listen.

I dash up the steps into the trailer. 'Zorro! Zorro!' But there's no answering bark. It's as quiet as the computer control room, as quiet as the toilets when Dinah disappeared.

No Steve resting on my bunk. No Zorro lying on the mat beside him.

'Steve!' No answer. I shiver. This is getting horrible. Everybody's disappearing . . . Virgil and Bella, Dinah, and now Steve. And Zorro! Where's Zorro? What if he's gone off somewhere? What if he eats something the Crowleighs give him?

There's a piece of paper on the bunk:

Dear Nicky, I waited for you, but I've got to find Dinah. I'm sorry, but she's my sister. Wait here, I'll be back. STEVE. PS Have taken Zorro, didn't want to leave him here on his own.

Have taken Zorro. He's got Zorro and he's gone off somewhere, not even telling me where. I am so angry I want to kick something. I kick the bunk as hard as I can, but it hurts me more than it hurts the bunk. Zorro. How dare he? Zorro's *my* dog. If Zorro's helping anyone he should be helping me.

I bang the trailer door shut and run down the track past the *BEARGARDEN*, which is full of little kids screaming as usual. I nearly fall over a kid who's lying flat on the path, screaming about ice cream. Both the parents turn and yell at me but I don't look back. Past the ice-cream booth, swerve round the *HOT DOG HUMDINGER*, short-cut through the *MYSTIC MAZE* and round the back of *SPACE RANGER*. I slow down here. All the cables run over the ground like snakes. It's fenced off so the Daisies can't get in but there's a way I know. It's dark and shadowy. There are cigarette ends on the grass, and drink cans. The screams from the ride echo like TV screams. I listen. It's OK, just the normal screaming. Nothing's gone wrong with *SPACE RANGER* yet.

Mack's office light is on. He keeps his lights burning all day, angled behind the scanner screens so they don't make shadows. I push his door open and he looks up, frowning, a bit annoyed to be interrupted but friendly too, the way he always is.

'Nicky? What's up?'

'D'you know where Bella and Virgil have gone? I need to talk to them.'

'Something desperate is it?' he jokes, smiling at me.

'Yes,' I say. 'It is.'

Mack stops smiling. 'You all right? No-one's hurt, are they?'

'No, not yet. But they will be – I know they will. That's why I've got to tell Virgil and Bella.'

'But they're not here. Didn't you know? A TV company rang this morning – one of those new ones. Sirius, was it? No, Capricorn. Said they wanted to interview them for a programme which goes out live this lunchtime. You've seen it. *Weekday Walkabout*. Virgil said would it be all right if just one of them went to the studio, but the TV people said it was both or nothing. And of course, it's all free publicity, so they went.'

'When are they back?'

'Search me. Depends how long it all goes on, I suppose.'

'Have you got the number? The number of the TV company?'

'They didn't leave it. Wait a minute, that's easily found out.' Mack picks up the phone and presses in some numbers. When a voice answers, he asks, 'Give me the number of Capricorn TV, would you? I don't know – Manchester, isn't it? Yeah. Thanks.' He scribbles down the number, and presses more buttons. 'Can you put me through to the *Weekday Walkabout* Studio please? This is *SPACE RANGER* at Mere Park. Yeah, they're doing an item on us.' I stare at Mack in admiration and he winks back. '*Weekday Walkabout?* I've got a message for two of your contributors. Virgil and Bella Damiano. Yeah, *Virgil and Bella Damiano*. Shall I spell it out for you? What d'you mean, they're not there? They've left already? . . . What d'you mean, you weren't expecting them? It was you who asked them to come in for an interview! Is that *Weekday Walkabout*? Oh. I see. Right. Must be some mistake. Sorry to have troubled you.' He puts down the phone, his face grim.

'Someone's made a monkey of us. Virgil and Bella went all that way for nothing. Capricorn TV never rang this morning. It was some joker.'

I stare at Mack. It's all fitting together. They took Dinah so Steve and I would be out of the way looking for her. And it's happened again. Someone has got Virgil and Bella out of the way.

'Mack. I don't think it was a joke.'

'What d'you mean? Do you know something about this, Nicky?' Mack glares at me as if I was the one who phoned in the message, pretending to be Capricorn TV.

'It's the Crowleighs. I know it is. They're trying to muck up *SPACE RANGER*. That's why they got Bella and Virgil out of the way, so they couldn't look at the computer and see what was going on. And they kidnapped Dinah. And Zorro's gone too, and I don't know where he is. And the computer program's going wobbly—'

'Hey, hey!' Mack holds up a hand like a traffic policeman. 'Let me catch up with this, Nicky. You think the Crowleighs are out to make trouble again?'

'Yes, they are, that's why they kidnapped Dinah and—'

'Whoa! Kidnap? This is major stuff you're talking about here, Nicky. Are you sure? Who's Dinah?'

'She's a little girl I know. She went to the toilet in the café and a woman with a baby pretended to be her mum and took her away. It was to stop me going after the Crowleighs. And they said they were going to kill Zorro.'

But Mack is looking at me, frowning. It's not a look I like. It's the kind of look teachers give you when they come over to sort out a fight and you start telling them everything that's happened, right from the beginning. A look that says, '*I'll listen to you and then I'll make up my own mind how much I believe. Because all this can't possibly be true*.'

'Hey, now, steady on,' says Mack. 'Killing Zorro, kidnapping Dinah, busting *SPACE RANGER* . . . The Crowleighs have had a busy morning, haven't they? Are you quite sure about all this?'

'Yes! Yes, I am! If Virgil and Bella were here they'd believe me, I know they would.

They know what the Crowleighs are like.'

'And I don't? They're trouble, don't think I don't know that. But you're talking serious crime here. It's not a game, Nicky.'

'I know that! Please, Mack, *please*. Come and look at the computer, the one that programs *SPACE RANGER*. You'll see what I mean.'

'Nicky. Have you been in that control room this morning? While Bella and Virgil were away?'

'Well, yeah, I had to, you see, because—'

'Didn't I hear Virgil tell you never to go in there without one of them?'

'Mm, but this is different, Mack, I had—'

'You haven't touched those computers, have you, Nicky?'

Mack stands up. Suddenly he's huge and stern, not the Mack I know. I'm going red, I know I am. I take a deep breath. I wish I had Zorro with me.

'Only to check something.'

'*Check something?* Nicky, what've you been doing?'

'I told you. I had to check one of the functions. Mack, someone's messing around with *SPACE RANGER*. I had to.'

'Yeah,' he says. 'Someone's been messing around all right. And I think I know who.'

But by now I'm angry, too. It helps me to find my voice and say, 'Then if I'm a liar, where's Zorro? Where's Dinah? Where's Bella and Virgil?'

He looks at me for a long time, then says in a quieter voice, 'I didn't say you were a liar, Nicky. I think you just got things mixed up, that's all. And you know you shouldn't have touched the computer. I'll have to tell Virgil and Bella about that.'

'Tell them! I don't care. I'll tell them myself. *They'll* believe me, I know they will.'

'Hey, listen, Nicky, I thought you and me were friends.'

But it's no good. He doesn't believe me. He's not going to do anything. Then I have an idea.

'Mack. If something's wrong with *SPACE RANGER*, it'll come up on your video scanner, won't it?'

'Yeah, 'course it will. That's what I'm here for. Early warning system.'

'Go through it now. Please. Check it now.'

There are video cameras all along the ride. Some of them are fixed focus, others keep swivelling, a bit like security cameras in shops. A lot of the ride is in darkness so we have infrared cameras too. I watch the images come up on screen as Mack presses the camera panel buttons. Three, four, one, seven . . .

'I'll make a composite tracking image,' he says. I know what that is. It's when all the angles are mixed together to give a complete picture of the ride. I can't interpret the pictures the way Mack can, but looking at the screen with him I can see the thrusters, the boosters, the rocket, the backdrops, the laser projections, the whole beautiful jigsaw of sound and light and space and distance that makes up *SPACE RANGER*. Mack brings up image after image onto screen. Suddenly he freezes one, pores over it, lets the images run on for a moment, freezes the picture again.

'Just a minute. I'm going to rewind on this one. Camera ten.' The images whizz back. Slowly, frame by frame, Mack plays it forward again. Then he shakes his head. 'No, seems OK. Thought there was something a bit funny about the speed there, but it's within the norm. I can't see any problems, Nicky, and I've checked all the cameras.'

'Maybe it hasn't started going wrong yet,' I say desperately. 'But I know it's going to. I saw it on the computer.'

Mack faces me. 'Those control computers, they're complicated things. I don't understand them myself. But they know what they're doing.' He smiles at me, kind but a bit sorry, as if I've made a fool of myself. He doesn't believe me. He's not going to help me. I turn away without saying anything.

'Nicky, where are you going?'

'To the entrance. To wait for Virgil and Bella.'

'Nicky!—'

But I've gone before he can say anything else. He thought I was making stuff up. I won't think about Mack any more. I've got to think of what to do next. Zorro. That's what I'll do next, I'll find Steve and Zorro. They can't have gone far.

But I don't have to find Zorro, because he finds me. I'm still round the back of *SPACE RANGER*, kicking a Coke can, trying to think where Steve can have gone, when I hear a yell:

'Get out of it! Go on, get!' and then a growl, a deep growl, way down in the throat, the kind of growl a dog gives when it's warning you that it doesn't want to fight but it will if it has to. I know that growl.

'Zorro!' I scream.

Eight

Zorro bursts on me like an explosion.

'Zorro! Zorro, boy! What is it? What's wrong?'

I drop down on my knees and put my arms around his neck. He's panting. If only this was one of those stories where the dog grabs his owner by the sleeve and drags him straight to where the trouble is. But it's not a story and Zorro does nothing but press against my legs, panting and shivering.

'Did someone try to hurt you, Zorro? Are you OK?'

'This your dog, is it?'

I look up. A big sloppy man in a baseball cap is standing there, staring angrily. 'You want to keep this animal under control, or I'll have the police on to you. He came running right through our picnic. Ruined my wife's best sherry trifle.'

Sherry trifle! He must be nuts. Who brings sherry trifle to a theme park?

'Cream all over her new dress. And who's going to pay the dry-cleaner's bill, that's what I'd like to know? I've a good mind to send it to your dad.'

'He's dead,' I say. That usually shuts them up.

'Oh. Very convenient, I must say.' He takes a step towards me, and Zorro turns. He growls at the man and shows his teeth, just a little.

'Get a lead on him!'

'All right, all right. We're going. He's only growling 'cos you shouted at me. If you kept your temper he'd be fine.'

'Come here, you little—'

But we're gone. I can run faster than a fat slob like him, and anyway, I know lots of back ways.

'Zorro! Where's Steve? Where've you left him?'

But Zorro doesn't tell me. We're running towards the entrance. It can't be long before Virgil and Bella come back. Then everything'll be all right.

I'm running as fast as I can, Zorro lolloping beside me. I'm hot and sweaty and out of breath and it seems as if this awful day will never end. And there suddenly, yelling and waving at me from the bench outside the Ladies' Toilets, is Steve.

'Steve! Where've you been?'

'He found you! Brilliant, Zorro! Hey, Nicky, Zorro found you just like in books.'

'What d'you mean?'

'I told him to get you. I couldn't leave here. They're in there, Dinah and that woman. I saw them go in. The baby was screaming and they didn't see me because I ducked down behind that rubbish bin. Hurry up, Nicky, you can go in there. They've been ages already.'

'Yeah, but what do I do?'

'Get Dinah, of course.'

'What if she won't come?'

'Tell her Zorro's out here. That'll make her come.'

'OK. Mind you're right outside. If you hear me yell, come in.'

'I can't go in a Ladies'—'

'YES, YOU CAN!'

But when I get into the toilets, Dinah's done her disappearing act again. I wait while three cubicle doors open and three strangers come out. I check the washbasins and the dryers. No Dinah. No woman and no baby. Of course!

There are two entrances to this toilet. She'd taken Dinah out the other way.

Just then I hear a tiny sound. A chuckly little noise from behind me. I spin round. There's a label on the door behind me that I've never noticed before. It says *Mother and Baby Room*. My heart bumps. That's where they are. Maybe she's keeping Dinah prisoner in there. Gagging her with a nappy. In spite of being frightened, I have to stop myself giggling. The little noise comes again. Very very slowly, I push open the door.

She's bent over the changing mat, talking to the baby.

'*Round* and *round* the garden, like a teddy bear, *one* step, *two* steps . . . '

There's no-one else in the room. Just the mother and the baby.

Everything's normal and nice, like in a nappy advertisement.

'. . . *One* step, *two* steps . . . ' The baby kills itself laughing and kicks its legs up in the air. The woman hears the door open and turns round, a big smile on her face. Then she sees me.

'This is the mother and baby room,' she snaps. 'What do *you* want?'

'Dinah,' I say.

Lots of things flicker in her blue eyes. Is

she going to lie to me, say she's never heard of Dinah? Then the big smile comes back.

'Oh, *Dinah*,' she says. 'You mean my friend's little girl. She's been helping me look after Eddie, hasn't she, Eddie? She's been playing peep-bo with you, hasn't she? Dinah's your friend.'

I don't know what to say. For a horrible moment I believe her. She's a friend of Dinah's mum, and she's been looking after Dinah for her. And I'm an idiot rushing round Mere Park telling Mack she's been kidnapped. Maybe there's an explanation for everything. Maybe I only imagined the wobble in the computer figures. Maybe it was just some kid playing a trick on Virgil and Bella, getting them to drive all that way to Manchester for nothing. Maybe none of it was anything to do with the Crowleighs.

'Um – where's she gone? Dinah, I mean,' I ask politely. The woman sticks down the tapes of the baby's nappy and peeks sideways at me through her long fair hair. There's a look in her eyes which I recognize. I've seen that look at school before, that little sideways, spiteful look. It's the kind of look someone gives when they think they know more about you than you know about yourself.

'Oh – she kept pestering me to have a go

on that *SPACE RANGER*,' says the woman. 'She kept on and on about it, so in the end I let her go. I've got a friend who works in the pay booth, so he let her jump the queue. She'll be up at the front by now.'

'But – but – she's only seven. She can't go on *SPACE RANGER* on her own!'

'Then she shouldn't keep asking, should she? It's her lookout, isn't it, Eddie? Dinah shouldn't be a naughty girl, should she? We all know what happens to naughty girls.'

'Why didn't you go with her?'

'Go with her? Oh dear, Eddie, we've got another silly girl here, haven't we? I can't take my little Eddie on that nasty *SPACE RANGER*, can I? 'Cos you never ever know what might happen, do you? You never, ever, ever know . . . '

She's not talking to Eddie. She's not even looking at him. She's watching me with that sly sideways look and laughing. *You never ever know what might happen* . . . What does she know? What does she know that she's not telling? I take a step towards her.

'Get back,' she says in a cold little voice. 'Get back or you'll be sorry.'

We stare at each other. I stare into her bright blue Crowleigh eyes and I find myself backing to the door, half a step at a time. Not too fast. I feel behind me for the handle, twist it.

'You'll – be – sorry,' she repeats. The baby isn't laughing any more. I pull the door open and get out as fast as I can.

'Where is she? Why haven't you got her?' Steve and Zorro jump at me.

'She's gone out the back way. That woman's let her go on *SPACE RANGER*. Quick! Something's going to happen, I know it is. We've got to catch Dinah before she goes on *SPACE RANGER*.'

'What do you mean, something's going to happen?' asks Steve.

I remember that Steve doesn't know about the computer. He doesn't know what I've seen in the computer control room, and tried to tell Mack. That something's going wrong with *SPACE RANGER* – badly wrong . . .

'They've hacked into the computer. They've altered the programming. *SPACE RANGER* is going to go wrong, I know it is.'

We look at each other. We don't say the words but they're in both our minds. *SPACE RANGER* is going to go wrong – with Dinah on it. And the Crowleigh woman knows about it – that's why she sent Dinah on the ride, on her own.

'Are you OK, Steve?'

''Course I'm OK.'

He doesn't look at all OK. Maybe he should stay here with Zorro while I try to find Dinah on *SPACE RANGER*. The thought of going on *SPACE RANGER* on my own now I know what's happening makes me feel a bit sick. But—

'I'll go and find her, Steve. You stay here.'

'You must be joking. She's my sister. Let's get going.'

We don't get going very fast. Steve's obviously feeling awful, whatever he says. I give him Zorro's collar to hold and Zorro half-pulls him along. But it's not far to *SPACE RANGER*. I can see the queue already.

'It's miles long! We'll never get to her in time,' says Steve.

'We're not going to queue. Come on, this way.'

I dodge round the barriers and the *2 hours from this point* and *1 hour from this point* signs. Zorro pushes through the crowd, with Steve close behind him.

'Oi, where d'you think you're going?'

'Here, there's a queue, you know!'

But we take no notice. We're both too busy looking for Dinah, but there's no sign of her. We're at the pay booth, and there's Joe Marr grumping at a Daisy who's given him a fifty pound note.

'Joe!'

'Oh. It's you.'

'Joe, have you seen a little girl? Long dark hair in a plait? I'm going on the ride. And this is my friend, Steve, he's coming, too.'

Joe drops the fifty pound note. 'Little girl? I haven't seen a little girl,' he says quickly. 'What're you going on the ride for? You've been on it millions of times. We're busy.'

But I know he can't stop me. I'm allowed on *SPACE RANGER* whenever I want. I know it, and he knows it. And I can bring my friends if I want.

'Three, please,' I say.

'You're not bringing that dog.'

'Virgil and Bella let me. You know they do.'

The crowd behind us is getting impatient. Joe bangs out three tickets from the automatic till. Then he looks up at me. There's something else on his face now, not just Joe's usual crossness.

'You'd better not go, Nicky.' It's half a plea, half a warning. As if he's trying to tell me what he can't tell me. Now I *know* I'm right. There's trouble on *SPACE RANGER*, and Joe knows it. He doesn't like me much, but he still doesn't want me to go on the ride.

'I've got to,' I say, staring straight back at him. He's put his hand down on the tickets so I can't pick them up. 'I've got to,' I repeat. Joe sighs. Slowly he lifts his hand up, and there are our tickets. I take them.

'Great,' I say, smiling at Joe. 'I'm really looking forward to it. I love *SPACE RANGER*, don't you, Joe?'

He gives a funny sort of grunt and turns away, to the next Daisy. And we're through.

Nine

Now we're in the Astrolaunch Tunnel, I remember when Bella and Virgil were designing it. They were worried about people getting hurt, shoving up behind each other in a narrow tunnel. And then there are lots of people who get scared if they can't see a way out of closed spaces. So it's all been planned. Once Joe Marr has given out twenty tickets, the till automatically shuts down until the 'through' light comes on, showing there is space in the tunnel. Each time *SPACE RANGER* is launched, there are eighty people on board, twenty in each of the four rocket sections. You have to feed your ticket into a barrier which is like the barriers at London tube stations. The machine gulps your ticket then slides it back to you as you go through the barrier.

There's just enough room for Zorro if he curls round. He's got his own ticket. The barrier cushions part to let him through.

'Shouldn't let dogs in here,' mutters a woman behind me.

'He's a member of staff, aren't you, Zorro?' I answer. 'He's a sniffer dog. Part of the security,' I add, and the woman says, 'Oh well, in that case,' and turns to tell her friend about it. It's so easy to tell lies. And so enjoyable.

'Why did you say that? About Zorro being a sniffer dog?' whispers Steve.

I wink, but Steve doesn't wink back.

We go on down the tunnel, Steve right behind me, my hand twisted in Zorro's collar. I'm never going to lose him again, not for a second. Every few metres there are slipways. If you suddenly realize you don't want to go on *SPACE RANGER* after all, you can step sideways into one of the slipways, go down another little tunnel and in a minute you find yourself back in daylight. MISSION ABORTED. Just ahead of us is the last barrier. Over it there is a sign: *If you want to get off SPACE RANGER, use the next slipway.* By the last slipway another big sign reads: *Final Exit. If you want to leave, LEAVE NOW!*

I want to slip sideways into that safe little tunnel to daylight. Ahead of us the grey, shiny, metallic tunnel stretches to the heart of *SPACE RANGER*. Once we're past here, there's no choice any more. We're about to go through the one-way door to the final section of the Astrolaunch Tunnel. Then we'll have to go on. Steve must have seen me slow down.

'You OK, Nicky? Listen, you can go back if you want. Dinah isn't your sister.'

I look at the door to the slipway tunnel. It's one of those soft rubber doors. So easy to push open. Zorro tugs against his collar but I don't know which way he wants to go. It's not just Dinah, though. It's *SPACE RANGER*. It's everything.

'What're you stopping for?' I ask Steve. Zorro pulls harder and this time I know which way he's pulling me. Down the tunnel. Down to *SPACE RANGER*, gleaming, humming with electronic energy, waiting.

I keep thinking I'll see Dinah. She can't be far ahead. But she's quite small and there's a solid moving line of people in front of us.

'I know she's here,' says Steve. 'She can't have got onto the ride before this. There wasn't time.'

'Let's call her.'

'No. Better not. You don't know who might hear.'

All those backs of heads. Any of them might turn. What if their eyes were blue, a hard, bright blue like the sun glittering on ice?

The tunnel divides into four smaller tunnels, each one leading to a different section of the rocket. Ticket numbers flash above each entrance. We are numbers 41–44. That means Tunnel 3. Suddenly, as the solid line of Daisies breaks up and swirls into its four tunnels, Steve grabs me.

'There she is! There! Going into Tunnel 1!'

I spin round but I've missed her.

'Dinah! Dinah!' Steve yells. His voice bounces against the smooth metallic walls of the tunnel. The echoes sound like someone laughing at us. 'Dinah! Dinah!'

It's too late. In a second Door 1 will slide smoothly shut, then it'll be sealed for the voyage.

'DINAH!'

And she hears us. A long time later she tells us what happens. Deep inside the rocket Dinah hears her name, and knows who is calling her. She acts as if she's known what to do since she was born. She's sitting in her seat but she's not strapped down yet, so she gets up and goes to the exit. She looks round quickly, checks no-one is near enough to stop her and jumps down into the tunnel again. She's alone. She listens until she hears Steve call her again. Tunnel 1 is empty so she darts back to the main tunnel and looks into Tunnel 2, sees it is empty and the door is starting to close. Runs to Tunnel 3, hears Steve's voice calling for one last desperate time: 'DII-NAAH!' and runs for his voice.

And makes it. Just as we reach the doors a small figure dodges between the legs of the boarding crowd and flings herself at Steve. She doesn't say a word, just grabs onto him as tight as she can.

'Quick! Get in!'

But the door bleeps at Dinah's ticket and won't let her past. She's at the wrong entrance. Her ticket is for Tunnel 1. A light flashes and words spring up on the electronic board above the door: *PLEASE BOARD AT GATE 1. PLEASE BOARD AT GATE 1.*

'Give me your ticket, Dinah!' says Steve. He throws Dinah's ticket on the ground. Then he crouches down. 'Get on. Piggyback!' Dinah hesitates. 'GET ON!' Then she clambers onto his back, wraps her legs tight around his waist, and her arms around his neck. He stands up and they both go through the door on Steve's ticket, with me and Zorro close behind.

'Brilliant! How did you think of that?'

'I've done it on the Underground,' says Steve.

We're in. We look at one another.

'Are you OK, Dinah?'

She nods.

'Why didn't you shout back when I called?'

'In case of that lady. Mum's friend.'

'How do you know she was Mum's friend?' asks Steve.

'She told me. But I don't like her.'

'Me neither,' I say. Dinah smiles, a small smile.

'Was she horrible to you?' asks Steve.

Dinah shakes her head. 'No. But I don't like her.'

'We've got to get in our seats. The lights are flashing,' I say.

There are twenty seats in our section of the rocket. 'Oh, no! There won't be a free seat for Dinah.'

'Can't she sit on mine? There's room for two if we squash up.'

I look at Steve. He doesn't know. He's a Daisy and he's never been on *SPACE RANGER*. How can he imagine what the thrust is like? Or how the rocket spins and twists through space? She'd get thrown all over the rocket. She's got to be in a seat, strapped down. The next minute the orange second warning light comes on. A computerized voice starts to issue instructions for strapping the five-point safety straps.

'She's got to be in a seat. Quick, have a look down there, Steve. There might be a space.'

But there isn't. There never is. There are three empty seats, one for each ticket-holder. One for me, one for Steve and one for Zorro. And the doors will shut thirty seconds after the orange warning. I look around desperately. I can't let Zorro go. But Dinah – we can't leave Dinah. Steve can't leave Dinah and I can't leave him. He's not well. He's just come out of hospital. Maybe he shouldn't even be on *SPACE RANGER* – let alone now, when anything might happen.

'Steve, you and Dinah get in those seats.'

'But—'

'STEVE! Strap her in quick.'

Ten seconds. Eight. I've got to do it. I grab Zorro and push him to the door. 'Go on, boy. Down! Down!'

He hesitates. Why am I telling him to leave me, in a place like this where everything smells funny and there aren't any trees or grass or bones?

'Go ON, Zorro! Down! Don't worry, boy, we're coming back. Wait here! STAY!' And as I say it the doors start to slide shut. I give him another desperate push and this time he seems to understand. He stops resisting me and with one smooth bound he is off *SPACE RANGER*. He lands in the tunnel, turns, stares at me, then lies down, head pointing towards the rocket where I am. I can see from his eyes that he understands. He's going to wait, however long it takes. The door closes. There's a hiss as the vacuum seal tightens. He can't hear me now but I call again, 'Wait here, Zorro! STAY!' In a minute the safety sensors will sweep to check there's no-one left in the tunnel, but with Zorro lying flat on the floor they won't pick up his image.

The red warning light is on. My eyes are fuzzy. I'm nearly crying, but not quite. I feel my way back along the rocket to the row of seats where Steve and Dinah are already strapped in. I know the routine of *SPACE RANGER* so well I could do this in my sleep. Sit down, lie back, feel the seat fall smoothly into flight position. Click the belt buckle once, twice. Shut my eyes. Squeeze the tears back, don't let them fall. Don't think about Zorro, think about *SPACE RANGER*. It's not the end of the journey, it's only the beginning. The red warning light goes off, and the first number of the countdown appears in the electronic panel above it. Ten. Nine. Eight. Countdown to launch.

Ten

'FOUR . . . THREE . . .'

The lights go dim. *SPACE RANGER* gathers itself like a horse ready to take the biggest jump of its life. There's a huge surge of power as the engines rev. The rocket tips, slowly, majestically.

'ONE . . . *ZERO!*'

I've forgotten how it roars. How the sound hits you like a wave, getting into every cell of your body and shaking it until it feels as if you'll be shaken to pieces. And when you think you can't stand it any more the sound goes on getting louder and louder, filling your ears and mouth until you can't even hear your own screams. I'm pinned down, my head on the head pad, pushed back into it by the giant thrust of *SPACE RANGER*'s launch. I can't move my head. I can't speak. Is this where it's going to happen? Have they altered the thrust so *SPACE RANGER* goes on and on accelerating until it shakes itself to pieces? No. No. Don't let it be that. I can't see anyone. I can't see Steve or Dinah. And there's no Zorro beside me. Through the windows there's the reflected glare of the rocket burners. It looks as if we're in hell.

And then the boosters come on. Two giant hands push me from behind. My head is forced back. I feel a wide stupid smile spreading on my face. I don't want to smile but I can't help it. It's the G-force. The whole world is roaring and shaking but I'm being lifted up, out of it, safe and free.

Suddenly everything stops. The rocket is full of tingling silence. The giant hands that have held me let go. I am weightless. If I wasn't strapped down I would float. Very slowly I turn my head, and there is Steve's face. It's got a big grin on it.

'Wow!' he says. 'Wow! I never thought it'd be this good!'

Dinah peeks at me from the other side of Steve. She's smiling, too.

'Look, Nicky! Look at that big blue and green ball!' She points out of the window. Our Earth is swimming away through space like a football someone's kicked so high it goes way over the heads of the crowd, and vanishes. Everyone in the rocket is pointing. But it's quiet. People whisper. You can't talk in an ordinary voice when you are watching our Earth like a jewel in the black velvet box of space, disappearing into a forest of stars.

'It's going!' says Dinah.

'Look, Dinah, there's England.'

But England is too tiny for us to see it any more. Europe melts into a splash of blue. Continents are wrapped up in clouds. Earth is as small as an egg now. As small as a drop of water. Gone.

'Steve!'

'It's OK, Dinah. It hasn't really gone. We're still here, on Earth,' says Steve confidently. Then he looks at me and whispers, 'We are, aren't we?'

''Course we are.' But huge space presses in at the windows, and stars flash fire.

'I don't know these stars,' says Steve. 'They're not like the ones in our sky.'

'I think we're out of the solar system now. Look, Dinah! Look at that red star!'

Dinah makes me feel braver. This is the bit I don't like, the bit where we're out of sight of Earth. My stomach begins to squeeze itself tight. My heart bumps but I make my voice sound normal.

'It's lovely, isn't it, Dinah? All those stars.'

'I want to see where we live,' says Dinah. She sounds as if she might cry.

'How long does it go on?' whispers Steve.

'Not long. We turn round soon and go back.'

I don't tell Steve that no ride on *SPACE RANGER* is ever quite the same as the last one. Virgil and Bella have built in what they call '*random variations on the ride*'. That means that there's a detail which is different each time. The route changes. Once we went so close to the moon on the way back that I could count the craters. Once we passed another spacecraft, going home, on its way back from Mars. No-one can ever say they know everything that happens on *SPACE RANGER*.

'I wish it'd go on for ever,' Steve says, 'but Dinah's tired.'

I look at Steve. The starlight on his face makes him look much older, and far away. He's relaxed and comfortable. I can tell he isn't frightened at all, not like me. He looks as if he belongs here.

I look out at the stars. There's a big greenish one, like Venus, only it isn't Venus. We are way beyond the solar system now. I've never seen this star before. We're going a long way. I glance at my watch. Four minutes. We should be turning now.

But *SPACE RANGER* goes on, rushing smoothly through weightless space at a speed I can't begin to imagine. Maybe this is just a new variation. A round trip. Any minute now I'll see the familiar planets. My hands are tight on the arms of my seat.

'What's the matter, Nicky?'

'I'm not sure. It's just – this ride's going on a long time.' I hear a wobble in my voice, like the wobble in the computer figures.

'Longer than normal?'

'Yeah. I think so.' Our whispers are so quiet Dinah doesn't hear them. She is staring out of the window, her eyes big. I glance cautiously round. It's OK. No-one else knows what to expect, so they're not worried. They think they're having a wonderful long ride. Good value for money.

Suddenly the curtain of stars goes ragged, as if something has bitten holes in it. Big gaps of dark appear. And more dark, and more dark. Soon we are surrounded by empty space. The stars are pricks of light, growing small behind us.

'Where are we now, Nicky? What's going on?'

'I don't know! I don't know, Steve! This has never happened before. Something's going wrong, I know it is.'

My voice is squeaky, but now I don't care if Steve knows I'm frightened. I've got to get out of this awful silent dark which is deeper than any night I've ever known. I want to run. I want to bash at the doors till they open. This isn't real. We aren't lost in space. We're only on *SPACE RANGER*. Outside there's Zorro and sun and grass and our trailer and a queue of Daisies. It's not real. It can't be real.

And then a computerized voice breaks the electronic hum inside our rocket section.

'*Attention please! Attention please!*'

Heads turn towards the speakers, eager for what's next. They think this is all part of the ride they've paid for.

'*A fatal error has occurred*,' the voice continues smoothly, '*resulting in a terminal malfunction of SPACE RANGER. Please wait for further announcements*.'

'What's going on?'

'What's she say?'

'Did you hear that?'

'Fatal error . . . '

'I don't like the sound of that.'

'Where's the emergency exit?'

Voices rise around us. Dinah reaches for Steve's hand. He turns to me.

'Quick, Nicky, say something!'

'Me? What d'you mean?'

'Yes, you! It's your ride. You're a Damiano, aren't you?'

Two kids opposite us have started to cry. I clear my throat. A little squeezed voice comes out. 'Um, it's all right—'

'NICKY!'

OK then, Steve, I'll show you. *SPACE RANGER* is ours. No-one's going to wreck it. I clear my throat again and shout as loud as I can.

'It's OK! It's just part of the ride! It's all part of the ride! There's no problem!'

Everyone's looking at me. The computerized vocals start up again: '*A fatal error . . .*' but I shout over it: 'It's just a recording! Part of the ride! I've been on *SPACE RANGER* millions of times and it's always like this.' They want to believe me. The frightened voices die down into mutters.

'That'll keep them quiet for a few minutes,' says Steve.

'What're we going to do? It's just going on and on. It should be back on Earth by now. I told you the Crowleighs had mucked up the program. I told Mack but he wouldn't believe me.'

'Right, let's think. Is there an emergency exit?'

'No. Once *SPACE RANGER*'s launched, you can't get off. That's why there are all those notices.'

'We could break the door down.'

'Yeah, I suppose so.' But what if we break down the door and instead of the safe world we come from, there's the empty mass of space? And we fall for ever and ever, drifting between the stars like dolls. No-one would ever know where we'd gone.

It can't be true. *SPACE RANGER* isn't real. It's just a ride.

I should have made Mack believe me. He knows *SPACE RANGER* isn't just a ride. It's a huge, powerful thing. Virgil and Bella know what to do with all that power, and make it work for us, but no-one else does. The Crowleighs only know how to destroy things.

'I can't see any stars,' whispers Steve.

'Nor can I. Isn't it horrible?'

'Horrible . . . No, not really. I like it.'

'You must be nutty.'

'No, I really do. It's so huge, and quiet. It goes on and on for ever. Nothing bad happens.

It's nothing to be frightened of. Dinah likes it, too, don't you, Dinah?'

He smiles at her and she cheeps back, 'Yeah, I like it!'

'That's because she doesn't know what she's talking about. And nor do you. You're just a Daisy.'

'OK, OK. The Crowleighs are bad, the Damianos are good. Daisies are stupid and Nicky Damiano knows everything.'

I am so embarrassed I forget to be frightened. Is that what I sound like?

'I only meant – you don't understand *SPACE RANGER*.'

'And you do? Right then, tell me what's going on. I'd like to know.'

'You do know. It's the Crowleighs—'

'Oh yeah. Those Crowleighs again. Well, if Bella and Virgil are so great, why aren't they doing something? They made this thing, didn't they?'

'They will do something, as soon as they know what's going on,' I say. I sound surer than I am. Why did Virgil and Bella have to go off like that? They should be here, now, looking after *SPACE RANGER*.

The smooth computer voice fills the rocket again. '*Attention please. Stand by for announcements*.'

We wait.

Sounding pleased and calm, the voice announces: *'The malfunction has been further identified. There is a complete loss of navigation of SPACE RANGER, with the result that we are now lost in space. End of announcement. Thank you.'*

There is a flurry of nervous laughter in our section.

'They make it real, don't they?'

'It'd have you worried if you didn't know it was part of the ride.'

'Amazing what they can do with computers these days.'

Yes, I think, quite amazing. More amazing than you know, luckily. I look round and smile at the other passengers. 'All part of the ride!' I repeat.

'They're not going to keep on believing me for long. They're not stupid!' I whisper to Steve.

''Course they are. They're Daisies, aren't they?'

There's no answer to that.

Eleven

The next part of the story belongs to Zorro. That makes it hard to tell, because Zorro doesn't see things in words. I have to try to make myself into Zorro, see what he saw, listen to what he heard and go where he went.

When the door of *SPACE RANGER* shut, with me on the other side, I left Zorro with nothing but the word *STAY!* Of course he knew what it meant, but when I told Zorro to stay, I thought I'd be back in less than five minutes, the time it normally took *SPACE RANGER* to make its journey. I wonder what time feels like if you never use a watch or a clock?

Five minutes passed, then ten. The next batch of Daisies had come down the Astro-launch Tunnel, and were waiting. Already the queue back by Joe Marr's pay booth must have been getting impatient. And Joe would have been checking his watch. He knew something, but not enough. He was on edge, worried and a bit frightened, too. He'd had his money to say nothing, and he'd said nothing.

Zorro waited and waited. He didn't like the shiny tunnel which smelled of metal and electricity. He'd seen the rocket tilt and slide away down the rails into the dark, then he'd heard the thunder of the launch coming out of the darkness. Dogs know when something's wrong long before humans do. They can sense when an earthquake's coming. Deep in his throat, Zorro began to whine. He could sense something he didn't like. And then he got up. He shook himself as if he was trying to shake off a bad dream. It's easy to guess that, because I know what Zorro does when he's worried. He lifted his head and sniffed and listened. And then, as if he'd heard something he didn't like, he whined again. Suddenly, as if he'd made up his mind, he turned and launched himself back up the tunnel towards the entrance.

A dog can get where people can't. It's impossible for a person to turn back from *SPACE RANGER* once he or she has passed the final slipway exit, but Zorro did it. He jumped the barriers. I know that because everyone was talking about it later on.

'A huge black dog. Must have been a circus dog, the way it jumped. Never seen anything like it.'

Joe Marr saw Zorro. He shouted after him, 'Oi, stop that dog!' but no-one did, and I'm not surprised. No-one would want to get in the way of a dog like Zorro. Zorro bounded past the pay booth, weaved round the line of Daisies and ran. Joe Marr couldn't leave the booth and go after him.

He didn't go to our trailer. He already knew there was no-one there. He was racing across the stretch of bald, trodden-on grass by the entrance when Virgil and Bella, hot and tired and cross, drove through in the van.

'All that way for nothing!'

'A whole day wasted.'

'We should never have gone. TV people think they can click their fingers and you come running. Bella! Look, isn't that Zorro?'

Bella braked. Zorro racing around without a lead and without me was bad news.

'Zorro! Zorro, boy, come on, what's the problem? Virgil, he's trembling. Something's wrong.'

'Better find Nicky.'

But Zorro wouldn't come in the van. He stood his ground and when they tried to pull him in he showed his teeth.

'I'll get out and go with him,' said Bella. 'You park the van. There's something strange going on.'

It was very, very lucky that Virgil and Bella are not ordinary adults, who think that everything is normal until proved otherwise. They believed Zorro straight away when he tried to tell them something was wrong, even though he hadn't any words. You can tell a story without words. Zorro whined, and ran a little way, then looked back at Bella and whined again.

'Come on, then, show me.'

She thought I'd had an accident, she said later. She was half-afraid to follow him. But he didn't take her to the trailer. Instead, he led her straight as an arrow to the entrance of *SPACE RANGER*. By this time Virgil had parked the van and was running after them.

As soon as Bella got to the pay booth she saw something was wrong. A crowd of Daisies was bunched up, grumbling. The red light by Joe Marr's till was on. That meant no-one else could enter the tunnel, because it wasn't clear. 'What's wrong, Joe?'

'Bit of a problem,' mumbled Joe, staring down at his automatic till.

'Have you checked the status of *SPACE RANGER*?'

'Still in flight.'

'What do you mean, *still*?'

I'd have been frightened of Bella when she looked like that, her face blazing. Joe Marr was, too. He mumbled a bit more about 'a bit of a delay', but Bella cut him short. 'There are no delays. *SPACE RANGER* is programmed. What's the report from the video scanners?'

'Um – I haven't checked that out yet.'

'*You haven't checked it yet?* Right. Give me that phone.'

Zorro knows when there's anger in the air long before human beings do. He picks up my feelings before I even know that I feel them. He must have stood there, tense, trembling with excitement. Had he done the right thing? Did they understand? Could he rely on Bella? Because human beings are so slow. They can't help it. A dog can smell danger but a human being can't. Zorro smelled danger when *SPACE RANGER* didn't return.

Bella picked up the phone and tapped in Mack's extension number. He answered straight away, as if he'd been waiting for it to ring. Later on he told me he'd been feeling bad since I left. He had a niggling worry that he ought to have come to the computer control room with me to check those figures. Maybe there was something wrong . . . But he couldn't leave the video scanner. And then he forgot about it, because suddenly he had his own problem. Instead of images of *SPACE RANGER*, the video screens frazzled into black-and-white snow. He adjusted all the controls, but he couldn't get the pictures back. Must be an electrical fault, Mack told himself. Maybe a storm somewhere. But it had never happened before, and Mack was getting really worried now. He remembered what I'd said. Could it possibly be true? Could someone get into the control computers, into the heart of *SPACE RANGER*? Could they alter the program? Something was blocking the pictures from *SPACE RANGER* so that they couldn't reach his screen. Anything might be going on out there! His fingers were frantic as he flipped the control buttons, but no pictures came up.

And then the phone rang. 'Mack. It's Bella here. Listen, we've got a problem. *SPACE RANGER* should be back by now but it's still in flight. We're not getting any information, just the red light. Run through the last few minutes on the video replay for me, would you? Check for any abnormalities.'

Mack's words fell over themselves. 'I can't. There's a problem here, too. Could be electrical. I can't get any images of *SPACE RANGER* at all. The screens are all blank, just snowstorm coming up.'

Bella turned to Virgil. 'Mack's not getting any images. This is serious. Let's get to the control room.' Then she spoke into the phone again. 'Mack, we're going to the control computer. We'll stay in touch by phone, OK?'

'Wait! Wait! Listen, Bella. Nicky was here earlier.'

'Nicky was? Do you know where she's gone? Zorro's here on his own.'

'She said she thought there was a problem with *SPACE RANGER*. She gave me a lot of stuff about the Crowleighs getting into the program and altering it. I didn't take much notice. I mean – it sounded ridiculous.'

'Where is she? Where'd she go?'

This is where Zorro knew it was time to act again. He heard my name. He knew where I was. He seized Bella's hand in his mouth, gently, the way he does with friends. He tried to tug her in the direction of the entrance tunnel.

'Hey, Zorro! Wait, boy, we're trying to find Nicky.'

But Zorro whined and pulled again, harder. Bella looked at him. Then she said to Mack, 'Hold on, there. I'll get back to you. Keep trying to get those pictures,' and she crouched down in front of Zorro and looked into his eyes.

'Zorro, do you know where Nicky is? Take me to Nicky.'

'I'll get to the control room. You go with Zorro,' said Virgil, and Bella nodded without taking her eyes from Zorro's. Virgil and Bella never need to explain things to one another. Each of them seems to know what the other is thinking.

Virgil was gone, running towards the computer control room. Bella straightened up and spoke to Joe Marr.

'Don't let anyone else through yet. I'm going down the Astrolaunch Tunnel to make some checks.'

'Oh – um, right. I'll keep the barrier up here.' She noticed Joe wasn't looking at her. He seemed strange. But she put the thought away. There wasn't time to worry about Joe now. He was always difficult.

* * *

The people waiting at the pay booth were getting restless.

'Here, what's the hold-up?'

'We've been waiting hours.'

'Are we ever going to get on this thing?'

Bella flashed them a huge smile. 'Half-price rides for the first hour after this is fixed,' she promised. 'Just a little glitch in the computers. We'll soon have you on.'

The grumbling died down. Half-price was a good deal, worth a bit of a wait. Bella thought quickly. There'd be people waiting around the exit for their friends to come off *SPACE RANGER*. But they wouldn't be getting worried yet, because the queues were always long and the wait was hard to predict. She needn't worry about them yet. Bella took hold of Zorro's collar and put the masterpass that she and Virgil always carried into the barrier ticket-slot. It slid open, and she walked through, into the empty, humming world of the Astrolaunch Tunnel.

Virgil was already at the computers. He bent over the screens like a mother bends over a sick baby. Something was wrong with *SPACE RANGER*, they already knew that. The question was, how bad was it and how quickly could it be fixed? Virgil never doubted that it could be fixed. He knew computers the way other people know their own hands and feet. At once he spotted what I'd seen. A bubbling, floating mass of figures where there should be a tight column plotting the trajectory of *SPACE RANGER*. It was worse than when I'd seen it, and it was getting worse every minute. His first thought was that there'd been a computer crash. But he didn't see how that could be. The computers were protected by the latest devices against variations in electrical current, power failures and tampering by unauthorized people breaking into the control room. And he already knew no-one had broken in. The locks were undamaged and the alarm system hadn't gone off. Then he thought of a virus. Had a virus got into the computer somehow? It was a million to one against. He and Bella ran a scrupulous programme of virus checking on any new software.

Hackers? Some computer expert way off in Manitoba or Moscow, who'd managed to get into *SPACE RANGER*'s program? But again, it wasn't likely. What motive would they have?

Then Mack's words ran through his mind. *'Nicky told me a lot of stuff about the*

Crowleighs getting into the program . . .'

Virgil knew the Crowleighs. He knew they believed *SPACE RANGER* was ruining them, taking away all the customers they might have had for their own rides. They had a motive, all right. And there'd been reports of the Crowleighs hanging around again, the past few days. Virgil had been wrong, he'd thought the Crowleighs were after information about the new ride. He'd believed they were trying to get into the workshop to discover what Virgil and Bella were planning next. But now it seemed they weren't interested in *THUNDER AND LIGHTNING*. It was *SPACE RANGER* they were after. A shock of horror ran through Virgil. The Crowleighs were right. If they could sabotage *SPACE RANGER* there'd be no point in the Damianos starting to build *THUNDER AND LIGHTNING*. Their rides would all be closed down because they were too dangerous.

But he was sure they didn't know enough about computers to get into the program for a ride as complex as *SPACE RANGER*. And then he thought again. The Crowleighs might not know enough about computers – but they had money. They could buy the services of people who did. People who knew enough to get into the program via their own computers and modems. It wouldn't be impossible.

'I should've thought of it,' Virgil muttered aloud, scanning the figures. It didn't take him more than a couple of minutes to discover that the alarm system on the computer had been switched off, too. No time to find out who or how. What mattered was to get *SPACE RANGER* back on course. What was the best way? Run the back-up program? No. That wouldn't be safe. He had to find the point in the program where *SPACE RANGER* had started to go wrong, and restore what had been damaged. Then, with any luck, *SPACE RANGER* would come back on course.

As soon as she was out of sight of Joe Marr and the waiting queue, Bella ran. She was down the Astrolaunch Tunnel, through all the barriers to where the tunnel split into four. She chose Gate 1. There was the launch pad, empty. The silence was ghostly. It should have been full of voices. *SPACE RANGER* should have been back on the launch pad. The rocket doors should have been open to let off the stream of people who had just been on the ride. They should have been heading for the exit tunnel, excited, ready to tell their friends about *SPACE RANGER*.

But there was no-one there at all. The silvery metal of the launch pad glistened under the harsh lights. *SPACE RANGER* had disappeared, with everyone in it.

Zorro whined. His fur rose on the back of his neck.

'All right. I know. But we'll find them. She went on *SPACE RANGER*, did she, boy? We'll get her back.'

Zorro whined again, his nose pointing into the darkness where *SPACE RANGER* had gone. His body quivered.

'We can't stay here,' said Bella. 'We've got to get to the computer control room and see what's wrong. Come on, boy.'

Zorro didn't want to leave. 'Zorro! Zorro! Come and find Nicky!'

He looked around and whined again. He wasn't moving, not now. He'd shown Bella all he could show her. Now he was staying here till I came.

'All right, then. Stay. On guard, Zorro!'

Bella looked back as she ran towards the exit tunnel. There was Zorro, alone in the gleaming silence of the launch pad, waiting for *SPACE RANGER*. She knew he wouldn't move.

Twelve

Inside *SPACE RANGER*, time has stopped. We lie there, staring out of the windows where there's nothing but the emptiness of space. Everybody is very quiet, but it's not a calm quietness. The atmosphere has changed. Tension is building up. A mother two rows away has her arm tight around her son, and he looks up at her with scared eyes. No-one asks any more questions. They don't want to hear the answers. No-one jokes any more. We are alone, cut off from the world, sealed inside *SPACE RANGER*. Someone coughs, and coughs again, nervously clearing his throat. But nobody speaks.

Steve notices it first. He whispers, 'Nicky, is it me or is it getting warmer?'

My hands are sticky. I thought it was

because I was frightened, but no. He's right. It's much warmer. Warmer than it should be. Fear flashes through me. What if there's a fire somewhere we can't see? What if the metal of *SPACE RANGER* is slowly heating up like an oven? No. Don't be stupid, Nicky. Look at all the fire precautions. Sprinklers and blankets and extinguishers everywhere. The sprinklers come on automatically. There can't be a fire. My fear dies down, then flares up again.

Sealed in SPACE RANGER. The doors are sealed. It doesn't matter normally, because the flight is so short. But there are twenty people in here, all breathing and sweating and using up air. What about the ventilation system? I listen, but I can't hear the reassuring drone of the air-pumps. And there's no cool ventilation draught on my face. That's why I'm hot. There's no air coming in. The Crowleighs don't know what they're doing. They've mucked up the program and they don't realize they've mucked up the ventilation, too. It must be a mistake. They wouldn't want us to be trapped in here without air, would they? Not even the Crowleighs would do that. But you don't have to be clever to destroy things. You don't even have to know what you're doing.

'Yeah, you're right. It's hot,' I whisper back.

All my thoughts have flown through my head in seconds. Should I tell Steve? I've got to tell someone!

'Steve. Don't say anything, but—'

'What? What's wrong, Nicky?'

I can trust Steve. He won't scream and shout so everyone panics. 'I think they've mucked up the ventilation. There isn't much air coming in.'

'What d'you mean? How much is coming in? Where does it come from?'

'The ventilation grilles. Don't let anyone see you looking. They're right above us. Above all the seats.'

'Oh. Right, I can see them. I didn't know what they were.'

'Can you feel any air blowing out of them?' A wild hope shoots through me. Maybe it's just my grille that isn't working.

But Steve slowly shakes his head. 'No. I can't feel anything. Nicky! Does that mean there's no air coming in at all?'

'Well – not much.'

Suddenly Dinah turns round from the window. 'Steve, Steve! I feel funny.' Her face is pale. Her forehead is sweaty and bits of her fringe are sticking to her skin. 'I feel sick,' she whimpers.

'No, you don't,' says Steve firmly. 'Shut

your eyes, Dinah. Think about a lemon. A big fat yellow lemon, all juicy. Pretend you're squeezing it and drinking the juice. *I always say that when she gets carsick*,' he whispers to me. 'It usually works for a bit.'

Dinah shuts her eyes. She doesn't look too good.

'We've got to think,' he goes on. 'What about emergency exits?'

I shake my head. 'There aren't any. It's too dangerous to exit from *SPACE RANGER* anywhere except the launch pad, because of the pressure and stuff. I don't really understand it, but I know that's what Virgil and Bella said. They said there were so many fail-safes built into the computer that emergency exits weren't necessary. And *SPACE RANGER* passed all the safety tests.'

'Not this one, it didn't,' says Steve grimly. 'Right. No exits. Where do we go from here?'

He looks awful, too. Worse than Dinah, but he doesn't seem to notice. Perhaps it's because he's used to feeling ill.

A mutter is starting in our section. Uneasy, fearful voices.

'Hot . . . '

'It's very hot in here—'

'Too hot—'

'I can't breathe.'

'There's no air.'

'Can't get my breath.'

Someone starts to cry. I don't know what to do. Should I say my bit about it all being part of the ride again? Is anyone going to believe me this time?

And then a thin, high, panicky voice from the end of the section shouts, 'Get us out of here! Are you listening? Get us out of here!' and the boy near us starts crying and Dinah whimpers and clutches Steve and I'm frightened, so frightened and—

—And a voice floods in through the speakers. Not the pleased-with-itself quack of the computerized information system. A live, warm, human voice. Bella's voice.

'Ladies and gentlemen. Please listen. You will be aware that there is a problem on *SPACE RANGER*. We are trying to correct your course as soon as we can.' She pauses, then says in a voice that sounds as if it's meant just for me, 'Don't be afraid. You will be free very soon.' Her voice breaks up into sighs and crackles. She must be using emergency radio contact, not the direct information channel through the computer. She says something more but we can't hear it. I strain forward in my seat, trying to catch her words.

'Two-way – Nicky – panel – fourteen.'

'Did you get that, Steve? What does she mean?'

'Two-way – does that mean two-way radio? Is there one?'

'I don't know.'

'Fourteen. Seat fourteen? Under seat fourteen? Do you think she means it's under there?'

'Behind a panel! That's what she means!'

'OK. Let's go for it.'

I am already dragging at my seat belt. The shoulder harness slips off. I am cramped and my fingers are shaking.

'Dinah!' says Steve in a fierce whisper. 'Don't you move. Stay here. Nicky and I are going to fix something so we all get back quick.'

Dinah gives him a scared nod. 'All right.'

The harness slips off and I stand up. I have to hold the backs of the seats hard. I'm weightless, floating. No, I'm not. I'm not really in space, for heaven's sake. I'm only on *SPACE RANGER*. My legs feel like this because I've been sitting still so long. All the same, I hold tight to the seats, and Steve and I move forward down the narrow body of the rocket. I've never walked round *SPACE RANGER* when it's in flight before. It's been drummed into me a hundred times that it's too dangerous. Eighteen pairs of eyes watch us, craning to see what we're doing.

Steve says, 'Please stay in your seats. We're activating the emergency radio to get help.'

His voice is strong, almost adult. I'm not surprised when people do as he says. No-one gets up. The crying has died away. We can hear hisses and crackles from the speakers, and a jumble of Bella's voice, but we can't make out any words now.

'Hold on to this. Here. This is fourteen. But where's the panel?'

We kneel by a pair of Doc Martens. Their owner shifts them to one side. Steve peers into the darkness under the seat, holding tight to the seat handle. The floating feeling is getting worse.

'There's a button on this panel – do you think that's it?'

'Try it.'

Steve pushes the button right in but nothing happens. 'Maybe it slides,' I say, and this time, as he slides it to the left, the whole panel moves. A tiny light comes on in the interior, showing knobs and dials and a tiny grille, a little bit like a ventilator grille. Steve wriggles forward.

'I can't see what these knobs are for. Here, Nicky. You're smaller. You could get closer.'

I crawl under the seat. My legs hurt. The weightless feeling makes them seem swollen. There it is, a bright dial, some arrows—

'I think I turn it on this way. Clockwise.'

'Well, go on, then!'

'OK – I'll try a quarter-turn first.'

The knob clicks. Another light comes on, this time a green one.

'There's no telephone thing to pick up. How do I talk into it?'

'I don't know, do I? Try just talking.'

It's getting hotter and hotter. My fingers are slippery on the knob.

'Um, it's me. Nicky. Can you hear me?'

But there's no answer. Only hisses and crackles from the speaker.

'What're you doing? Nothing's happening, Nicky.'

I'll have to try something else. Cautiously, I stretch to the big dial and twist it a little way. Static crackles through the rocket. I jump back, then touch the dial again, twist it the other way, slowly, slowly, as if I'm tuning in to a radio. And then I hit Bella's voice.

'Nicky, can you hear me? *SPACE RANGER*, are you receiving me?'

'Yes! Yes! Bella, it's me!'

'Nicky! Great, you've found the transmitter. OK, everybody, we've got two-way contact.'

I'm not sure if she's speaking to us or to people back there in the computer room. She goes on. 'Nicky, tell me what you can see from the windows right now.'

'I can't see anything. I'm under a seat. Wait, I'll ask Steve.'

But he's heard, of course. Everything Bella and I say is being echoed round the rocket by the speakers now.

'It's still dark, Nicky,' says Steve. 'Tell her it's just space.'

'We're going through darkness, Bella. No planets. No stars. Just nothing.'

There's a pause, then Bella's voice again. 'That's what we thought. OK, we're trying to get you back on the course you left. It shouldn't take long.'

I lean towards the grille again. Then I remember. I can't tell her, or everyone will hear. And then that awful crying will start again. Only worse. People might freak out completely if they hear about the air.

'Bella,' I say quickly, 'you remember when I used to have to take that Ventolin? Remember why I needed it?' I know she'll remember. I used to get asthma, and Ventolin helped me breathe. I don't get it any more, but right now being in *SPACE RANGER* reminds me of that struggle to get air into my lungs.

'Yeah?' says Bella. 'Listen, Nicky, we haven't got time for that—'

'Bella.' I'm praying no-one else in here has asthma and knows about Ventolin. 'I need my Ventolin. I need it now.' Is she going to understand? Is she going to understand I'm trying to tell her that there isn't enough air in here? Please, Bella, *please*. Listen to what I'm saying. Don't make me have to spell it out.

I hear Bella's breath go in sharply. She's got it. She's understood.

'O-K,' she says slowly, 'I get the picture. I'll be back with you in one second, everybody, hang on.' The radio goes dead. She'll be talking to Virgil, telling him what I've told her. *They're running out of air*.

Do something, Bella. You've always known what to do. You and Virgil made *SPACE RANGER*. It's your baby. There's nothing you can't do with it. Get us home. Just get us home.

It's probably less than a minute before Bella is back, although it seems like an hour. Her voice is fresh and bright.

'OK, everyone. Plan B. We're taking a shortcut home. Now I want you to listen carefully because this is a change from the usual program. *SPACE RANGER*'s going to do a flipover and cut back through space.

Now there'll be a lot of shaking and noise but don't pay any attention. *SPACE RANGER* is built to take it. You'll see all kinds of stuff out of the window as well but just imagine you're watching a firework display. We are about to override *SPACE RANGER*'s program and bring you home. Check your safety harnesses. Press your heads back into your seat pads. Nicky, get back to your seat right now. Leave the radio. HURRY.'

I'm out from under seat fourteen. Steve drags me upright and we struggle through the thick, hot air back to our seats, clinging to our handholds. I can hardly move. It's hard to breathe. It's getting worse every second now and there's a tight band round my head, pressing in, squeezing hard. Fumbling, we get our safety harnesses back on. Steve puts his arm right round Dinah, and she hides her face against his sleeve. Bella's voice comes again.

'Ten seconds to override. Wait for the flipover. Push against your seat as you feel the thrust. Three. Two. One. NOW!'

And the thrust comes, like nothing I've ever felt before. It's not outside me, it's inside, in every particle of my body. The thrust builds and builds and builds. It's too much. Nothing can stand it. The panels rattle and the lights flicker and go out. We are alone in roaring, stifling darkness. The pressure is still rising. I can't move. My whole body is being bent double, forced through a tiny gap which won't take it. My head's going to fall off. I try to scream, 'No! No!' but I can't make a sound. Orange tongues of flame lick at the windows, followed by a storm of white flashes that tear into the darkness of space. *SPACE RANGER* heaves like a whale caught on a harpoon. Then there's another sound. It's a groan, a cry out of darkness, like the cry of a whale as it dies. We feel *SPACE RANGER* turn on itself, shuddering, and break the lock of space.

And then silence. Floating. It must be like this after you die. Maybe we *are* dead. Everything's gone. The pressure and the shaking, the howl of *SPACE RANGER* as it tore itself out of its course. All gone. There's nothing to struggle against any more. The lights have come back on, dimly, and they show rows of quiet people, lying back, staring at the roof of the rocket. Everyone's face is calm and peaceful. The radio is silent. We must have lost contact.

'Look!' whispers Steve. 'Look!'

Far off, so far off I can hardly see them, a swarm of bright pinpricks is drifting towards us.

'Stars!' says Dinah. 'I can see the stars!' And she beams at us. It's still hot but somehow it's easier to breathe.

'I can see them, too,' I say.

Soon they are all around us, glittering through the windows. Other worlds, not empty space. We aren't alone any more. *SPACE RANGER* is limping home through a forest of stars.

'We didn't come this way,' says Steve, pointing at a huge orange star with belts of deep red around it. 'We never saw that, did we?'

'Well, if it's a shortcut, like Bella said . . .'

'I think it's OK,' says Steve. 'I'm sure it's OK. It feels right.'

We glide on. It's dreamlike, as if someone is hauling us through water by an invisible thread. Planets whirl faster. Suddenly, from up the rocket, there's a shout.

'Earth! Earth! Look! It's Earth!'

And they're right. It's as small as a Christmas tree decoration, but it couldn't be anything else but Earth. In all space I've never seen any other planet like it. Blue and green and perfect. As we look, it leaps towards us. Now we can see how fast we're travelling. We can see the oceans, the continents. It's getting huge. It fills the windows. What's going to happen? We've never re-entered this fast. *SPACE RANGER*'s program must be racing. What if the shock blows it apart? *SPACE RANGER* tilts, swings. I tense myself for the bruising shock of re-entry. And now *SPACE RANGER* is bathed in fire as we roar into the friction of the Earth's atmosphere. I can't watch any longer. I reach out, grabbing at nothing, and maybe the air gives out or I faint, but my eyes won't open any more. I fall back into the dark.

Thirteen

'Nicky! Nicky!'

I know that voice. Got to get to the radio. Bella's voice. Can't see anything.

'Nicky!'

Someone's shaking me. Got to get up. Must be late. My head hurts.

'Make way, please. Make way. Stretcher here!'

Another voice. A big, comfortable, man's voice.

'You're all right now, Nicky. We're going to lift you. One. Two. Three.'

I feel myself held safe, lifted, set down. Something warm and soft is tucked in around me.

'Steady!'

I'm being lifted again. Carried. My head

feels better. I try to clear my throat, say something, but the words won't come out. Bella's voice again.

'You're OK, Nicky. Don't worry. We're just taking you for a check-up.'

My eyes open a slit. I can see! It's Bella, it's really Bella, not just her voice. She's walking along beside my stretcher, one hand on the red wool blanket that's tucked in around me. And beside her, padding like a shadow, eyes fixed on me, so close I can touch him, 'Zorro!'

'It's OK,' says Bella. 'Zorro's here. He waited for you. Don't talk now. I'll tell you what happened later. Everybody's fine.'

I drift off into a peaceful place behind my eyes.

When I next open my eyes I see a flowery curtain. Suddenly it swishes back and a woman with a stethoscope comes in, beaming. I don't need to ask her where I am. I spent a lot of time in hospitals with Dad.

'Where's Bella?' I demand.

'She just went to make a phone call. Well, *you* look a lot better. Let's check you over again.'

She checks my breathing. She holds up fingers and makes me count them. She asks me to remember who the Prime Minister is, and what I had for breakfast.

'We might do some X-rays. And I want you to breathe into a peak-flow monitor later. But you look fine to me.'

'Was I hurt?'

'You passed out from lack of oxygen. Let's hope there wasn't any brain damage!' She grins and I smile back. 'Somehow I don't think there was. But don't try to get up just yet. You might feel dizzy.'

'Did everyone pass out?'

'No, just you and the boy – Steve, isn't it? You were moving around, weren't you, sending messages on the radio? That took up more oxygen than lying still. We've checked everybody else and they've been allowed home.'

'How's Steve? Where is he? Can I see him?'

'Um – well, maybe not just yet.'

'He *is* all right, isn't he?'

'I'm sure he'll be fine. His mum's with him now. And his little sister. You can see him later.'

The doctor smiles again, reassuringly. Sun is coming in behind my head, pouring onto the white sheets. I turn my head and look at the clean blue sky and the treetops waving in the summer breeze. Our green and blue planet. Home. It is wonderful to be back.

'Here she is now. Your mum.'

I don't bother to say that Bella isn't my mum. There she is. Seeing Bella is like coming home, too. She sits down by my bed and the doctor slides out through the curtains.

'Where's Zorro?'

'Right outside. Tied to a tree in the courtyard. He knows you're in here.'

'I can't wait to see him.'

'It won't be long.'

Bella looks exhausted. She's still wearing the clothes she must have put on to go to the TV Studio – a big T-shirt with the *SPACE RANGER* logo on it in black and glowing silver, and her black and silver leggings. The logo has a 3-D effect. It would have looked amazing on screen.

'Is Virgil with you?'

'No, he's still sorting things out. There are safety inspectors and police all over the place.'

'I don't know what happened.'

'Do you remember when I told you on the radio that we were going to override the program? That's what we did. But you had to re-enter the atmosphere without orbiting first, because the oxygen was so low. We were getting the figures that there were only a few minutes to spare. So it was a rough re-entry. You passed out, so did Steve.'

'What about the rest of them?'

'Not too bad. Pretty frightened.'

'We'll have to give them some free rides to make up for it,' I try to joke, but Bella doesn't smile. She rubs her eyes hard, as if she's trying to rub something away, then she says:

'There won't be any more rides.'

'What do you mean?'

'*SPACE RANGER*'s burnt out.'

'What, the program? Or do you mean the rocket?'

'Both.' She is silent for a moment. I have never seen Bella cry. She is a fighter. But there's a sadness that is worse than any crying in her face.

'You can mend it! You can build it again! I know you can!'

'We can't, Nicky. That's what it took to override the program, smashing it back like that, through space and time. *SPACE RANGER* won't fly again.'

'Oh, Bella.'

'I know.'

We are both quiet. Bella takes my hand, gives a little smile. 'We got you back, though.'

'Those Crowleighs. I could kill them!'

'What good would that do?'

'They tried to kill us. All of us. We'd have died.'

Bella shrugs. 'I don't think they meant that to happen, Nicky. They didn't know what they were doing. They didn't know the first thing about *SPACE RANGER*. But they can't make things, so they just destroy them.'

I stare at Bella. I remember the silent emptiness of space, and the roaring fire that bathed *SPACE RANGER* when we re-entered the Earth's atmosphere. Does anyone understand *SPACE RANGER*, except Bella and Virgil? And maybe me, now, just a little . . .

People think that *SPACE RANGER* is just a ride. All done with lasers and computers. Wonderful effects. Virtual reality. But of course you don't really go into space. That's impossible.

Or is it? The more I know about *SPACE RANGER*, the less I know.

'*SPACE RANGER* is finished,' says Bella firmly. 'And that'll keep the Crowleighs quiet for a while. Think of the publicity we'll get after today. The headlines there are going to be. *Lost in Space. Air Runs Out on Danger Ride.* Just wait for tomorrow's papers. We'll be on TV all right now. Oh, the Crowleighs are going to think they've killed us off.'

'Will they close us down? Won't we be able to do rides any more?'

'They might try. There'll be an inquiry for

sure. But we'll say the locks and seals jammed because of vandalism. They'll never be able to prove otherwise. We'll say there are new safety checks so it can't ever happen again.'

'But if *SPACE RANGER* is burnt out, then it doesn't make any difference, does it? The Crowleighs have won.'

Bella laughs and her eyes sparkle. She doesn't look at all like someone who has been killed off.

'It's terrible,' I go on. 'No rides. What are we going to do?'

'Did I say no rides?' Bella leans forward and whispers, 'We're one jump ahead, Nicky. You've got to be like a lizard. If they grab your tail you let them have it and grow a new one. The Crowleighs don't know about *THUNDER AND LIGHTNING*. We were going to close *SPACE RANGER* soon, anyway. It was time for something new.'

'Oh!'

Something new. The words bubble in the closed cubicle. *THUNDER AND LIGHTNING*. The Stonehenge giant striding across the plain, lit by lightning flashes. The roar of thunder, the white and blue zigzag of lightning searing across the sky. It will be amazing.

And I will get five per cent.

'Can I see Steve?'

'Yeah. His mum's just gone. I had a word with her.'

Bella looks grim.

'Was she – is she in with the Crowleighs?'

'No. She didn't really know what was going on. The Crowleighs fooled her, told her all sorts of lies about how they'd give her the money for a new treatment for Steve, in America, if she helped them. Of course they wouldn't have given her a penny. But don't say anything to Steve. He doesn't know.'

'He *should* know! His mum helped the Crowleighs! We could have been killed!—'

'Nicky. Don't you think she's got enough to deal with? And maybe Steve has too?'

I flush and look down. My fingers pick at the thin hospital blanket. 'OK, then. I won't say anything.'

'Joe Marr's gone.'

'Where?'

'I don't know. He left a note. Said he was sorry, he didn't realize people were going to get hurt.'

Oh, well. Perhaps Joe Marr wasn't so bad after all. After all, he did try to stop me going on *SPACE RANGER* . . . Nothing's as simple as it seems.

'Can I see Zorro now, Bella? PLEASE!'

Bella glances round. 'I can't bring him in here. But it won't hurt if you get up for a minute. When I whistle, go over to the window. I'll bring Zorro round so you can see him.'

She disappears. I wait, my heart bumping with excitement. So much has happened that I can't take it all in. The fall through the dark – *SPACE RANGER* blazing as it hurtled through the atmosphere – everything is jumbled up, playing through my head like a fast rewind. My hands are clenched on the sheets.

Suddenly Bella's whistle cuts through the confusion. Slowly, carefully, I get off the bed, clinging to the metal hospital headboard as if I'm still weightless. I lean against the high windowsill and peer down. There's the courtyard, with the evening sun making everything golden. I squint against the light. They are there, the two of them, Bella kneeling by Zorro's side, waving and pointing upwards. Zorro's dark fur is tipped with golden points. He's looking at me. He's seen me. His head goes up, his tail thumps against the grass. And I wave back, blinking away the tears that make Zorro a blur of black and gold.

It's a while before they let me see Steve. First I have to have X-rays, then I breathe into the peak-flow monitor, and there are more tests to see if I'm brain damaged. I could have told them I'm not. Just because I got mixed up about who was Prime Minister . . . By the time I'm dressed in my own clothes and allowed to go along the corridor to the ward where Steve is, I'm really tired. He and Dinah are playing cards. They both look up.

'Steve!'

He looks all right. He looks fine. Much better than I thought he'd be. There's loads of stuff on the side of his bed, fruit and sweets and flowers. That's a waste when he'll be out again in an hour or so, like me.

Dinah launches herself at me and gives me a big hug. 'We thought you were dead, Nicky!'

'I am. This is my ghost.' Dinah lets go of me and backs off. 'I'm only joking, Dinah! Of course it's me.'

'She doesn't always know what's real and what's not,' says Steve.

Nor do I, I think, but I don't say it.

We all look at one another. I don't really want to talk about *SPACE RANGER*, and they don't seem to want to, either. It's all too close, too fierce. Too real. We'll talk about it some other time.

'When's your mum coming back to take you home?' I ask. I want to get out of the way before she does, so I won't have to see her.

'I'm not going home today,' says Steve,

picking up some cards and riffling through them.

He starts to deal them out on the blanket.

'But – you look OK—'

'They want to do some more tests. It's to do with my chemo, I think.'

'Oh.'

'There's a friend of mine in the next ward. Chris. He's back in, too.'

'That's nice.'

Steve laughs. 'Yeah, really nice!'

I blush, embarrassed. 'I didn't mean—'

'It's OK, Nicky. I'm used to it. The only thing I don't like is that you never get any peace. People are always banging round.'

Suddenly I remember how Steve looked when *SPACE RANGER* went out way beyond all our familiar planets, into deep, quiet space. I was frightened, but Steve liked it. He wasn't pretending. I can shut my eyes and see his face now, calm and peaceful.

'I'll come and see you,' I promise. 'I mean, if you'd like me to.'

'Yes,' says Steve. 'That'd be nice. If you're sure you've got the time to come and see a Daisy.'

'You aren't a Daisy. Not now.'

'Good.'

The lights are coming on. Suddenly darkness jumps to the windows. I can hear the new nurses arriving, the night nurses, calling to each other. Doors slam and a trolley comes clattering down the corridor. I know what Steve means about the noise.

'There's the moon,' says Dinah. She's sitting on Steve's bed, staring out of the window. We all look up. Silent, empty space is a million miles away, and as close as my next breath. In my head I hear the thunder of *SPACE RANGER*, making for the stars.

THE END

From the Carnegie Medal winning author...

WORLD-EATER
Robert Swindells

'There's something in the sky . . . something terrible!'

On the night of the great storm, a mysterious new planet suddenly appears in the sky. Orbiting the sun between Mercury and Venus, the huge blue-grey sphere has scientists baffled as probes reveal its surface to be flat and bare and its interior liquid.

Eleven-year old Orville, absorbed in waiting for his favourite pigeon to hatch her first eggs, is the first to suspect the true nature of the planet. But will anyone listen to his theory? And, if they do, can they avert disaster? For if Orville is right, the world is doomed . . .

0 440 86349 X